SHE DIES TONIGHT

AN ARTEMIS BLYTHE MYSTERY THRILLER BOOK 1

GEORGIA WAGNER

Contents

Prologue

Panic set in.

And so she dug.

One shovel of earth after the next. Speckles of mud flecking her sweat-slicked face and scattering across the ground cover. The scent of freshly turned earth mingled with the redolence of moss and detritus.

The shadow lingered over her shoulder, watching. His silhouette spread towards her like a puddle of ink.

Her hands were blistered. Her breath coming in scattered gasps. She needed to hurry—she knew that much. She needed to find *it* before her daughter returned home from school. She could picture little Sophie; her bright red, princess lunchbox swinging back and forth as she skipped up the long driveway. Had she packed Sophie's juice this morning? Donna couldn't remember.

So strange the thoughts that crossed one's mind when faced with death...

She was now knee deep in the hole she'd dug. As the sun shifted in the sky, winking coyly between the leaves and boughs, watching through the canopy in resplendent beams of gold, the shadow of the large house behind her stretched its arms to ensnare the two figures in the five-acre backyard.

"Faster," the husky voice demanded. She began to turn to protest, but the voice snapped. "Don't look at me!"

She went very still, swallowing slowly. Out of the corner of her eye, she spotted the long, sharp bowie knife he clutched in one gloved hand.

"How deep did you bury it?" he snapped.

"I—I don't know," Donna said, her voice shaking. She wanted to turn, to watch the intruder. Her spine tingled, wondering if—at any moment—the knife would find its mark. Off to the side, she spotted the smashed, sliding glass door the intruder had entered through. He'd grabbed her from where she'd been sitting in the lounge and threatened her.

So of course, she'd told him where it was buried.

She hadn't expected to actually have to *dig* up the thing.

Now, her arms ached. Her breath was fleeting. Mud-stained everything. The privacy of the five-acre lot, shielded by large oaks, had seemed a good idea at the time, when her husband had suggested it twenty years ago. The seven thousand square foot mansion, complete with a turret and private pool, had been the selling point. Especially given how Donna and her husband had grown up.

Now, though... she wished they'd just stayed in Seattle.

"Where is it?" the muffled voice demanded. "Where did you hide it?"

"I don't know," she said, her voice shaking. "I—It should be here... Right here!" Another shovel of dirt. A quick fling. But the hole was empty. Had she forgotten the spot? Had someone moved it?

She felt another jolt of panic.

She bit her lower lip, breathing slowly, trying to think. He only had a knife. She hadn't seen a gun. The shovel... it was sturdy...

Maybe... though she trembled thinking it... maybe she could hit him and run. The neighbors would hear her scream eventually. Wouldn't they? The Mitchells next door were also a private folk. They also lived in a very large mansion.

Yes... yes, she decided. She couldn't keep digging. He was growing impatient. She had wracked her brain to try and discern *who* this was. She thought she recognized the voice—but he was disguising it. Speaking in what sounded like an intentional rasp.

Her blistered hands tensed on the shovel, and she summoned what nerve she had. With one hand, she brushed her auburn bangs from her eyes. And then her foot scuffed something.

She frowned, glancing down.

A small, dark corner of a box jutted from the base of the hole. Her eyes widened. She gasped in relief. "Oh, thank God!" she declared. "It's here! I found it. Right here!" She felt a flush of sheer joy. The man had come for the buried box. Now, hopefully, if she gave it to him, he would leave.

"Let me see!" he demanded, stepping to the edge of the hole and peering down. The knife was still clutched in his good hand.

She pointed with her toe, scuffing more dirt and revealing the gleaming letters etched across the top of the container.

He nodded, his lips—visible in the opening of his ski mask—turning slowly. "Perfect," he murmured.

"You can have it!" she said. "All of it. Please... just... just..." She swallowed.

But she went still at the look in the man's eyes. They flashed behind the ski-mask. And then a faint, rattling chuckle emitted from the mask. "Oh... no, no," he murmured, shaking his head mirthfully from side to side. "I don't *want* it. I just wanted to know where it was."

"I—what?"

He started kicking dirt. Sending it into the hole. Covering the corner she'd just unearthed.

"Stop! Wait—stop, what are you doing!" she protested. "I thought you wanted it? Why—why did you have me dig it up?"

"So I would know where to bury you," he said simply.

It took a moment for his words to register. But then her eyes widened. She began to swing the shovel. But he moved far, far too fast.

The knife, little more than a silver blur.

1

Artemis Blythe's queen fell, and her opponent took it violently off the board. He hid a quick grin, stowing the queen with the other captured pieces near his elbow.

Artemis peered over her steepled hands, listening to the quiet *tick-tick-tick* of the chess clock at her side. She watched her opponent for a moment, studying his features.

"Look," an audience member spoke from amidst nearly two hundred spectators scattered throughout the room. The man stood behind a cordoning rope, whispering to a friend. "She's doing the stare, again. See—I told you."

"Hush," came the reply of an usher.

The voice quickly went silent. It was strictly forbidden to speak while in the viewing gallery, and most chess fans wouldn't want to miss the last game of the Seattle Open. Some suggested that the winner of this tournament would be the favorite for Nationals.

Artemis, though, was focusing on one tournament at a time. As the first woman to have broken the top 50 ranked grandmasters, she had more than the usual number of eyes watching her meteoric ascent.

It was *her* eyes, though, that often captivated the attention of the online bloggers and vloggers. Those same eyes now studying Stefan Wright. An older, seasoned veteran of the game. Currently ranked in the top 50 players in the world. And yet she watched him all the same with her mismatched gaze. Heterochromia iridium—one of her eyes was blue like moonlit frost, the other hazel-gold.

She studied her opponent's expressions, postures, body language almost as much as she studied the board. A flicker of the eyes one way, a twitch of a finger. Some thought this was a gimmick. A way to unnerve the opposition. The reality was far less mundane. She'd been raised by a mentalist—a man who'd trained her to notice every swallow, tick, widening of the eyes, blink...

She still remembered those lessons, cold-reading an audience. To Artemis, words were whispers. Physical motion was a scream. There were some who played the game of chess looking for the perfect move. But while, theoretically, Artemis believed in perfect moves in any closed system...

This wasn't theory. People were flawed, and people had preferences. Made mistakes. For instance, Stefan was in his fifties. He also, in the last five games, had frequented the restroom once every two hours on average. He would always eat pasta before the game.

And so, she'd decided to take him deep.

The longer the game went, the more he'd feel nature's call. The quicker his carb-loading would crash.

Games at the Seattle Open could take longer than six hours if needed.

So she'd started a defensive opening. Picturing the memorized movements in her mind. Everything playing out in her thoughts like a movie screen. She took her time about her moves, too. Especially early on.

She wasn't just playing the game.

She was playing Stefan.

And he had just fallen for the gambit.

The queen had been a poison piece. He didn't see it yet. He would have earlier. He had even been a stronger player in the first couple of hours... But barring checkmate, the game didn't end until she flagged or resigned. And now, the longer the game had gone, the weaker he'd grown. Six moves from now, she'd fork his king and rook. Then the skewer would come.

She'd already won, but he didn't know it.

She watched Stefan, studying the flick of his eyes towards the queen he'd captured then back to the board. *Count the pieces on the board. Never the ones taken.*

One of the rules her older sister—her first chess coach—had taught her. The game was going well; she couldn't wait to see what her favorite analysts, the Washingtons, thought of it.

She settled back, slowly glancing down at the board again. As her eyes shifted, though, something caught her attention.

A man waving at her.

She brushed her coal black hair behind an ear, biting a lip. Her pale skin, some suggested, was from too much time spent studying, memorizing, learning. Really, though, when out in the sun she never bronzed. She only burnt.

Porcelain complexion, black hair, mismatched eyes... Some of the more desperate fans in the audience would offer attention she preferred to avoid.

It was also one of the reasons people online hated her. Smart? They could take. Pretty? They would gaze at their screens in rapt attention when they thought no one was looking. But both?

Some loathed her for it. And so she dressed simply. Didn't wear make-up. Didn't wear jewelry. Soap instead of perfume. Her hair neat, pulled back in a simple ponytail. *One enemy at a time.*

Another one of her older sister's admonishments.

Artemis missed her sister. The blame for this, also, could be placed firmly at her father's feet.

Her mismatched eyes flicked back towards the man waving at her. *Tick-tick-tick.* The clock insisted upon her. But she couldn't focus now.

She recognized the man.

Not a chess fan.

Not at all.

In fact, the last time she'd seen him, he'd been sitting in a testing center, watching as she took the strategic portion of the FBI's preliminary competency exam.

It had been a marketing gimmick. Something her then-manager had cooked up to raise interest a few years ago on a much smaller stage.

She'd taken a MENSA test, a fluid IQ test and multiple personality tests. The public online, in the small chess community, had gobbled it all up. Like most grandmasters, she was classified as something of a genius. But the man across from her, Stefan, was also a genius. Most the men on the all-time list for chess were geniuses.

IQ did not make her unique in her field.

As for the personality tests, those results she'd refused to release to the public. Heavy on strategic thinking and future ideation. Heavy on doing the right thing. Extraordinarily competitive. And levels of suppressed neuroticism that manifested in the form of nightmares and panic attacks. Though these she'd managed to hide from most of her fans so far. She dreaded the day that one of the online vloggers found out she suffered panic attacks.

She frowned towards the man behind the velvet rope, who was still waving at her. He was gesturing urgently. Now that her gaze landed on him, he was tapping at a silver, blue-strapped skeleton watch just beneath his sleeve.

One of the ushers hurried over to the fellow creating the disturbance. The moment he approached, though, the man flashed his FBI badge. The usher hesitated, swallowed, then retreated to go fetch one of the tournament coordinators.

Artemis noted all of this with a rising sense of frustration.

She glanced back at the board. She moved quickly; pawn to b4. Another poison piece. But this time, Stefan went still. His grin flickered, fading. He leaned back, frowning.

Now he saw the trap.

But it was too late.

The best traps were the ones where, once the bait was tasted, there was no avoiding them.

The man standing behind the red rope was dressed somewhat casually for an FBI agent. He was taller than most of the spectators, with dark eyes and hastily combed hair. His socks, she noticed, didn't match. The same as she did with everyone, she studied him. Not just his face—where the eyes were usually drawn—but all of him. Mismatched socks. One of his shoes scuffed on the left side, suggesting he hadn't seen the curb from the parking lot. She'd nearly tripped there too.

The fingers on his left hand kept tapping in time with the *tick-tick-tick*. A scar traced the inside of his right hand. A thick, roping scar where it looked as if he'd tried to squeeze a hunting knife. A faint fleck of red on his jacket. Ketchup? She couldn't tell from here.

An unanswered question. She bit her lip again—a nervous tic. She hated unanswered questions. Then again, much of her life was one giant question mark.

The FBI agent with the tousled hair and scarred hand kept gesturing. He was now whispering. "Ms. Blythe. Psst. Hey." A few of the other spectators were now shooting him looks of fury. One man even nudged him with his elbow. Instead of reacting in anger, though, the tall agent glanced at the nudger, winked, and gently pushed the elbow away.

Then he returned right back to trying to gain Artemis' attention.

She glanced back at the board. Stefan had moved again.

She didn't hesitate. *His* queen had been forced to move. He'd brought it out too early, after all. She'd spent half the day hunting his queen. But now came the pivot.

Forget his queen. She wanted the win.

Knight to C7. Check.

Three moves left before checkmate.

Her opponent frowned, shifting uncomfortably now. He hadn't used the restroom in nearly two hours.

"Psst. Ms. Blythe," the agent whispered.

A few of the onlookers were glaring at him now. The tall man in the half-buttoned suit shifted, going quiet but still gesturing. There was a tattoo just visible past the collar of his shirt, creeping up under his neck. She couldn't make out the design from here. If anything, though, the man looked like he was playing professional—like some free spirit crammed into a suit against his will.

Artemis sighed. Stefan shook his head, muttering beneath his breath. "Good game."

Then he toppled his king in resignation.

"Well played," she said quickly, rising to her feet and extending her hand.

Stefan took it, if somewhat reluctantly. Whispers erupted from the spectators. A few of them were now glancing at the small TV monitors above the seating, watching as analysts broke down the last few moves. She nodded politely to her opponent, shook, then turned, moving over towards where the tall agent was still gesturing.

As she approached, she allowed a frown to curdle her features.

"What?" she said, trying her best not to snap. But the mental exhaustion of the day had already taken its toll.

He began. "My name is—"

"Agent Forester, I know," she said simply.

He blinked in surprise. "I…" he glanced down at his suit jacket, as if looking for a name tag. "I guess I have one of those faces," he muttered.

"I remember you," she explained quickly. "The testing center in Quantico? March 15th, three years ago. You were wearing the same suit, Agent Forester."

His lips nearly creased into a stunned smile, but he hid the expression of amusement as quickly as it threatened to come. "Ha, wow. Neat trick," he said, nodding congenially. Again, if he sensed the irritation in her tone, it didn't effect him in the least.

A few of the fans beyond the rope were now murmuring. Some were trying to pass annotation sheets for her autograph. Others were recording video with their phones. The tournament was over. The points were being tallied, but everyone already knew the result.

Artemis Blythe was the first woman to win the Seattle Open. Her ranking was now 2710. The number one player in the world was nearly 2900. No one, in history, had ever passed the 3000 mark. She was determined to be the first. Having just turned thirty, she still had time to make it happen. She hadn't even started on the tournament circuit until six years ago.

"Nice match—I've never played checkers before," the man said.

"Chess," she retorted but then realized he was joking. Her irritation levels were only rising. Who did this guy think he was? One moment he was interrupting her match, the next he was teasing. Though this second part seemed more a feature of the person than the moment. As if he simply couldn't help himself. His eyes were still twinkling, eternally amused at some unspoken joke.

Up close, she spotted things she hadn't noticed earlier. The red mark on his shirt wasn't ketchup. It was blood. She spotted a similar red stain just inside his left nostril. One of his ears was misformed on the left side of his face.

Despite this, he had handsome features which, aside from the mischievous veneer, communicated a similar urgency to the one found in his gestures and tone.

"Have you been fighting?" she asked.

He hesitated now, eyebrows rising. "Jeez. How the hell did you know *that*?"

"Training?" she guessed. "Boxer or martial artist?"

He tucked his tongue inside his cheek. "Now, I think you're just showing off."

She hesitated, considering this. "Perhaps," she said simply. "So, Agent Forester, what was so urgent you couldn't wait until after the final game of the tournament?"

"Oh, shit," he said. "I—crap. Really, sorry. I didn't know this was an important game. I was just told to get you."

"Why?" she said slowly.

Now, his tone sobered somewhat. He scratched at his misshapen ear—a fighter's ear. "Is your aunt's name Donna Kramer?"

Artemis went still now, staring at the agent. "No," she said slowly. "She was my foster mother for two years."

"Oh... Well, in her will it said—"

"She treated me like family," Artemis said. "What's wrong? What's happened?" She could feel the faint tug of anxiety twisting in her gut, congealing into a hard knot. The first sign of a panic attack. She tried to inhale slowly, forcing herself to calm.

But then, Forester said, "I'm very sorry to tell you... Your Aunt, er, foster mother was killed this morning. Could you come with me?"

She stared, wondering if this was his version of a sick joke. "Killed how?"

"I know it's shocking. I'm very sorry." Strangely, he seemed to mean it. He shook his head, running a hand through his already bedraggled, brown hair. "All will be explained. Come with me, please."

But he wasn't smiling now. He peered down at her, nearly a foot taller. He unhooked the velvet rope, lifting the faux-gold clasp and gesturing for her to duck under. "Please, Ms. Blythe. There are two other agents waiting downstairs. We're in a bit of a time crunch."

And this time, his insistent tone didn't leave much room for refusal.

Her stomach was twisting. Her eyes blinking, threatening to reveal tears. Donna was dead? That... that wasn't...

Artemis shook her head, her dark hair swishing.

"A-alright," she murmured, her voice shaking. "Alright. Just... let me grab my things."

2

Artemis sat in the back of an SUV with tinted windows. Agent Forester was driving, occasionally glancing in the rearview mirror. Another man, broad-shouldered and muscled, suggesting he spent a decent amount of time at the gym, sat in the front passenger seat, his expression bored but also masked by a pair of dark sunglasses.

The other figure in the vehicle, who Artemis was studying closest, was a pale-haired woman with the dangling emerald earrings.

The woman wore a neat blouse and smelled faintly of roses. Her hands were folded delicately over primly crossed legs. Though the woman couldn't have been younger than sixty, there was an elegance to the way she sat. Perhaps *confidence* was the better word.

The woman's two emerald earrings swished.

Artemis studied the woman quickly, doing a once over. No wedding ring. No tan mark on either ring finger. The emerald earrings were the sort designed to look better when worn than displayed, suggesting the woman had purchased them herself rather than having been gifted them.

Single, sixties, elegant... The way the two other men were acting...

"You're the boss," Artemis said at last as the vehicle picked up pace, leaving the convention center and moving onto the highway. "Alright, we've left. No paparazzi, no vloggers. So what happened to Aunt Donna?"

"I thought you said she wasn't your aunt," Forester called into the back.

"She isn't. I just call her... *called* her that." Artemis swallowed. "What's so important you couldn't tell me back at the center?"

The older woman glanced over. Her eyes matched her emerald earrings. Her chin and jaw looked as if they were fixed in a rigid, unmoving position.

"You are Artemis Blythe?" the woman said simply.

"I—yes..." Artemis frowned, her eyes darting between the three.

"Forgive my manners," said the woman. "I'm Supervising Agent Shauna Grant. You've already met Cameron Forester. And the silent gentleman is Agent Wade."

"We call him Ox," Cameron called cheerfully into the back.

"I'd like to say it's pleasant to meet you," Artemis said slowly. "But I'd prefer if you just answered my questions. Is my aunt really dead?"

"She is, I'm afraid," said Agent Grant. She pointed suddenly, "Take the next exit, Cam."

Artemis blinked at the familiar term. The tall man in the front seat didn't bat an eye but followed the instruction, sticking to the speed limit. Other vehicles zipped by them, but Forester didn't seem to mind. This, she decided, was a man who marched to the beat of his own drum. An easygoing, relaxed beat at that.

Agent Grant turned back, those emerald earrings swishing once more and catching the last rays of evening sunlight coming over the misty Cascade Mountains.

"So what happened?" Artemis said stiffly. "You said killed... but you mean *murdered*, yes?" She didn't mean to sound so detached, but a question had presented itself. A question no one seemed willing to answer.

The other figures in the vehicle shifted uncomfortably. Agent Cameron Forester shot a quick glance in the mirror, meeting the eyes of the supervisor.

"Did you mention—" Grant began, frowning back at Forester.

"Not a word," he said. "She also knew I'd been kickboxing. I think she's psychic."

"I'm *not* psychic," Artemis said fiercely. Her voice shook with anger. "There are no such things. Only charlatans. Pretenders." Her mind moved to her father once again.

"Damn, alright then," Forester said, nodding. "Sensitive topic. I get it. But you're wrong."

"Wrong about what?"

"There are psychics. I've met 'em," he nodded adamantly. "But look, there I go again, talking out of turn. My bad." He raised a scarred and calloused hand. "I'll be quiet now."

"No, you won't," muttered the second man from the front seat in a bored voice.

Forester tapped his nose and pointed at the second agent.

Grant, though, was frowning at Artemis. "I'd like to think my agents are able to follow basic protocol," she said, an edge to her tone. "But yes, I'm afraid your aunt was murdered."

"Forester didn't say anything," Artemis replied softly, her stomach twisting into a cold knot once more. She felt a lance of grief. It had been fifteen years since she'd seen Aunt Donna. But the woman had been kind to Artemis. A very, very rare experience during her childhood. She continued, her voice shaking, "It doesn't take a genius to figure out the FBI isn't here for someone who slipped and fell in the shower. So back to my original question. What happened?"

"That," said Grant, "is why you're here."

"Me?"

"Yes. You are... in a somewhat unique position to help us."

"I don't see how I can do that."

"Ah, so she isn't all-knowing," Forester quipped from the front seat. "I was beginning to think I might have to delete my browser history."

"I've seen your browser history," muttered Agent Wade. The buff man in the dark sunglasses gave a shake of his head. "Lot of shirtless men."

At a glare from Grant, Forester trailed off, muttering, "Cage fighters... Shirtless *cage* fighters... I'm a fan."

"You'll have to forgive Forester," said Grant primly. "He's ataraxic. He doesn't mean to be rude."

"Atar—what?" Artemis frowned. It was uncommon for her to encounter an unfamiliar term.

"Means I can't feel fear," Forester called into the mirror, grinning. "He tapped his forehead. No social fear. Very little physical fear. You know... Product of anti-social personality disorder."

"He's a sociopath," Agent Wade added. His tone was as flat and serious as ever.

Artemis blinked, her eyes darting about the vehicle, again wondering if she was being pranked. She hadn't known it was possible to pass an FBI psych-eval as a sociopath. Not unless Forester had some powerful connections.

"I'm sorry," she said slowly, frowning. "I don't understand what it is you wanted to speak with me about. I haven't seen Aunt Donna in nearly fifteen years."

"No," said Supervising Agent Grant. "We are aware of that. We also... have been looking into your background."

Artemis stiffened. She'd been worried this was why she'd been snatched up. She shifted uncomfortably in her seat, biting her lower lip and tugging uncomfortably at her seatbelt.

"I see," Artemis said simply. "You can't think I have anything to do with it..."

Grant didn't answer the question. Instead, she said, her voice stern, "There have been three murders in the last three days in a small town at the foot of the Cascade Mountains. This isn't the first time a serial killer has targeted Pinelake."

Artemis let out a shaky breath. "I'm *not* my father. Besides, I've been in a public tournament for the last five days. I couldn't possibly have anything—"

"We don't think you did it," Forester called. "That's the good news."

"The bad news," Agent Wade said, looking back at her and staring with his dark sunglasses, "Is your name was dropped."

"My name? Who? Did someone *say* it was me?"

"No," Grant replied. The woman pursed her lips. "Next turn up ahead, Cam."

As the vehicle merged, moving into the right lane, Artemis suddenly realized where they were going. She tensed, her hand bunching against her leg. She felt the familiar icy knot in her stomach and instantly started to calm her breathing, trying to suppress the rising tide of horror. "No," she said slowly. "No—whatever he told you, he's lying. He's a bastard. You have to know that."

"We do," said Grant, nodding once. Her hands were still resting lightly on her crossed legs. She tugged at the edge of her modest, calf-length, flared, beige trousers. "But Artemis Blythe, you have to see it from our perspective. You are the Ghostkiller's daughter, aren't you?"

"Did he say I did it?" she demanded, ignoring the question. "He did, didn't he? He's playing with you. He's using *you* to play with me. He doesn't know anything. How could he? He's been locked away for seventeen years."

"Locked where you helped put him, yes?"

"How is that relevant?"

"You were only twelve at the time. And yet you helped catch a murderer who killed seven young women—two of them only teenagers. I'd like to think you didn't know what he was doing. You didn't *help* him."

Artemis felt a stabbing, icy sensation. Her skin prickled. This part of her history was another reason so many of the fans online had cottoned onto her. The girl with the mismatched eyes... the Ghostkiller's daughter. She refused to answer questions about her father, though. About her childhood or the case.

This had only increased the mystery surrounding her. Had only encouraged the online chess community to speculate, unearthing any article or tidbit they could find in their incessant search for gossip.

More than once, she'd walked out of an interview or signed off of an online call when questioned about her past. Now, though, she was trapped in a car with three FBI agents. Storming out wasn't an option.

Carefully, her voice prickling, she said, "I've answered those questions two decades ago. I don't need to convince you."

"No. But you can't deny that you are your father's daughter. You share a connection."

"I don't share *anything* with him. I haven't seen him in eighteen years. And I'd like to keep it that way. So turn around, please. I want to go back to the convention center."

"I'm afraid that's not possible. Three women have been murdered in Pinelake. A killer is striking *daily*. We don't have time to waste, so we have to pull on *every* thread."

They were headed towards the federal supermax prison where her father was being held. She knew this because she'd specifically avoided the drive as often as possible. In fact, she'd avoided the Pacific Northwest for almost fifteen years. The only reason she'd returned for the week was to participate in the tournament. Her next stepping stone to Nationals.

She'd justified the decision to travel here for seven days under the auspices of a quick stop, a quicker victory, and a promise that she'd avoid two locations above all.

Her hometown of Pinelake.

And the prison where her father was incarcerated.

And now, by the sound of things, she was being dragged back towards both.

3

"What did he tell you?" she demanded. "He must have said something. What?"

"He said," Grant replied quietly, "That he knows who's committing the murders. But he refuses to—"

"Tell anyone except for me?" she demanded in exasperation.

"Damn, she's good," Forester muttered.

Agent Wade just grunted.

"No, just listen for a second," Artemis implored. "He's a liar. He's a con artist. He spent nearly twenty years as a charlatan, stealing other peoples' money."

"He's not in prison for theft," Grant retorted. "As you well know. You're the one who helped solve the case. You put your own father behind bars."

"I didn't know he was the one killing those poor women at the time," Artemis retorted. "I just spotted the discrepancy on the news and made a phone call. I didn't have a clue it would lead back to *him.* I was only twelve!"

"Yes, well... He says he knows who's killing in Pinelake. He says he'll tell only you. Three women are already dead, Ms. Blythe. Do you really want to sit by and let another die, knowing you could have helped?"

Artemis scowled, glancing between Forester's gaze in the mirror to Grant's prim, straight-postured form. "This isn't my job," she said firmly. "It's yours. And if you're here, willing to follow the say-so of a liar and a serial killer, then it means you have *nothing.* "

"Bingo," Forester muttered.

"Cam," snapped Grant.

"What? She's right. We've got shit all. Look, Artemis," Forester said, glancing in the rearview mirror once more. "Grant is bad cop. That makes me good cop. And Ox here is... well, barely a cop."

The dour-faced partner didn't react to the jab, like a boulder that had weathered many storms in its time.

"We're not *demanding.* We're *asking* for help. Alright? Pretty please with a cherry on top and sprinkles. Please. Women are dying." He spoke earnestly, nodding encouragingly as he said it.

"You're asking?" Artemis pressed.

He nodded.

"Then take me back to the convention center."

"Ah, shit. No can do, sorry."

"You said I had the choice!"

"I was lying. I thought you'd be willing to help. Alright, back to you Grant, I tried."

The supervising agent, shook her head apologetically. By the looks of things both her and Agent Wade had built up something of a tolerance for the easy-going, sociopathic agent's prattling.

But the look in Agent Grant's eyes was dead serious. "Artemis, we need you to speak with your father."

"I won't," she said simply, shaking her head. "I refuse."

"We need your *help*!"

"I have rights. You may have talked me into this car, but I have rights. We both know I do. You can threaten to detain me if you want, but let's see how two hundred thousand followers on my stream react to finding out the FBI kidnapped me."

"Followers on your stream?" Grant shook her head. "I'm afraid I don't know what that means. And you have me all wrong. I'm not trying to strong-arm you. I'm *begging*." Those emerald earrings kept swaying in mesmerizing patterns. "We're running out of options. This is our only lead."

Artemis hesitated, biting her lip again. She refused to speak to her father. That was a non-starter. No way in hell. But also... three women dead. Including Aunt Donna. Some bastard had killed the only woman who'd ever given Artemis a hug.

A strange statistic to know, but Artemis kept track of nearly everything. For thirteen years she hadn't known a mother's hug. Then for two blissful years she'd lived with Aunt Donna. The woman had moved to Pinelake only three years before the incident.

Artemis sighed.

She'd caught a killer before, hadn't she?

Besides... on that FBI practicum she'd taken, in the strategic portion of the test, she'd scored the highest marks possible. In fact, she'd even made some suggestions to improve the clarity on two of the questions. Though the proctor hadn't seemed amenable to the suggestions at the time.

Artemis let out another, longer sigh, staring down at her legs.

"I won't speak to him," she said simply. "But... but maybe I can help some other way."

"How is that?" Grant asked, her voice cold.

"I could help with the case. You take on CI's don't you? Or maybe a consultant. You don't even have to pay me."

"We don't *need* a consultant," said Grant firmly. "We need you to speak with your father and find out what he knows."

"Nothing. He doesn't know anything. He's playing with you and using you to get to me. That's what he does. He's a psychopath that plays mind games. He's a genius too. Allowing him to *speak* is your first mistake. Don't listen to anything he says. He's a devil. But yes, maybe if you let me see the crime scene, I could give some input."

She could tell Grant wasn't convinced. So she pressed further.

"I know Pinelake. I grew up there. I know the people, and many of them will remember *me.*"

"And you think the memories they have of you will be positive?"

Not at all, she thought. "Perhaps," she said. But even as she said it, she felt a faint shiver. Part of her wanted to demand she be let out. She could take a taxi back to the convention center. But someone had killed Aunt Donna.

She could still picture that night—she'd only been thirteen. Months after she'd placed the phone-calling spotting the mistake on the television. Her father led away in handcuffs, silent as the grave. His expression emotionless, his eyes moving like they always did. Surveying, cataloging.

She remembered standing there with her younger brother, Tommy. She hadn't seen him in nearly fifteen years either.

They'd watched from the porch as a female social worker began speaking with them about the group home where they were to be taken.

Artemis remembered crying then...

She could think of exactly two other times that year she'd cried.

Never again since. She didn't shed tears anymore. Refused to give in.

But she could remember the moon watching the two of them. Tommy a rail-thin, beanpole of a boy. Artemis silent, watchful like her father. She'd thought it a compliment for years when people compared her to him.

The memory stung.

And that's when Aunt Donna had shown up. Her son and Tommy had been friends in school. Had played football together. Donna had insisted the children stay with her.

Artemis could remember the swelling relief. She was going to be allowed to stay in Pinelake. Near her friends. At her school.

Their older sister had been killed two years before...

The murderer now walking away in handcuffs.

It had been such a mess.

But Donna had come to the rescue. Had taken them in as if they were her own children. Artemis had even had her first kiss in the Kramer household. Her brother's friend—Jamie Kramer. He'd had the most perfect sea-gray eyes. Whenever he looked at her, it was as if he could see into her soul.

He'd been an awful kisser, though. But so had Artemis.

Two years they'd lived with the Kramers. But it wasn't the reprieve Artemis had thought it would be.

Spray paint on the front door.

A brick through the windshield of Mr. Kramer's Mercedes. Someone had hidden a dead rat in the garage.

The message from Pinelake had been clear.

The Ghostkiller's children were *not* welcome.

Seven victims. Each plucked from the quaint suburban homes of the mountain-side village. Seven daughters and sisters and mothers and friends.

Pinelake wanted blood.

Over those two years, Artemis had heard her name whispered. Had heard the threats. Received phone calls, promising to kill the family.

Tommy had run away in August... And then Mr. Kramer had put his foot down. Two years was too much. The family wasn't in the position to keep Artemis.

He'd apologized profusely, of course. She could still see the look of guilt in his eyes.

She could remember Mrs. Kramer screaming at her husband in the parlor. Remember the tears.

But in the end, Mr. Kramer had his way.

She never had managed another kiss with Jamie. And so at the age of fifteen, she'd started bouncing around. Foster care. Group home. And then, at eighteen—emancipation.

She'd settled in Salinas, California for a few years. Chess had been an outlet. An online game. The only real tutor she'd trained with had been her sister... But when Helen had gone missing, Artemis had retreated even more fully into the game.

Books, videos, strategy guides, lessons, podcasts—she'd spent every waking moment studying the game.

A strategy she could control. A game that made *sense.* Pieces were lost, yes, but only in exchange for victory. The cleverer she was, the better she did.

No surprises. Not if she played perfectly.

And she'd learned, at a very young age, perfect play wasn't about the board. It was about the person across from her.

She'd taught herself for nearly a decade. And then, while moving from one odd job to another, making just enough part-time to afford rent so she could spend more time studying the beloved game, she'd played in an online tournament and won.

Five hundred dollars. More than she made after tax in two weeks of work.

And from there, over time, she'd made something of a name for herself in the circuit.

If not for Aunt Donna, Artemis wasn't sure what would have happened. Three years in the group homes and foster system had nearly killed her.

Four?

Artemis didn't think she'd have made it out.

Her brother, Tommy, she'd managed to track down. He was now living in Seattle. According to her source—a friend she'd met online—Tommy had some connections with the Seattle mob. At least he was still alive.

Unlike their sister.

Artemis had not lived an easy life.

But if someone had killed Aunt Donna... she couldn't help but remember the way Donna had fought with her husband. Screaming in the parlor.

Demanding they keep the children.

She'd lost in the end.

Mr. Kramer had his way. He couldn't take any more threats, bricks, dead animals, askance glances at church or the country club.

She didn't blame him.

She didn't think much of him at all.

But Donna had gone to battle for Artemis and Tommy.

She owed it to that woman to do the same.

She couldn't sit by and do nothing. Not while women like her aunt were being killed. And her father? He thought he was so clever... They all did. All these monsters who preyed on the defenseless. If her father so badly wanted company in that prison of his, she felt inclined to oblige him. Artemis was nothing if not competitive.

Another killer behind bars sent there by Artemis.

That was the closest her father would *ever* get to speaking with her again.

She nodded more adamantly. And then, knowing she had to play a card to cinch the deal, she said firmly, "If I can't find anything by looking at the evidence, or seeing the crime scene myself, then you have my word. I'll speak to my father."

Grant had been mid-protest until this last part.

Now, the older woman went quiet, her eyes narrowed, studying Artemis. Agents Forester and Wade watched in the rearview mirror, attentive, but momentarily quiet.

Grant sighed. "We have twelve hours before he'll kill again, given the recent MO. I'll give you one. One hour to find a lead. And if not..."

"We speak with my father," Artemis said quickly. "I swear it."

Of course, she had absolutely no intention of meeting the old man.

Which meant there was only one option. She had to find *something*. Some lead. Some clue. Something the FBI had missed.

She'd done it once before, eighteen years ago.

Now, twelve-year-old Artemis Blythe, the Ghostkiller's daughter, had turned into the thirty-year-old grandmaster. Strategy was strategy, wasn't it?

The same skills she used to study her opponents. Cold-reading, body language, intentions and emotions and all in between...

It would help.

It had to.

Not only was she determined to find a lead the FBI had missed.

She also would get justice for Donna.

And as for her old man? He wasn't half as clever as he thought he was.

To prove this, she was willing to return to Pinelake. Willing to face a town that scorned her family's name. A place she'd sworn she'd never step foot in again.

4

He watched from the side of the mountain, standing amidst the fir trees. Low wisps of mist teased down the slopes, trailing along his form. He raised the binoculars with one hand, half-seated on the rocky outcrop pattered with moss.

He shifted into a more comfortable position, watching the comings and goings of his latest burial site.

He couldn't help but smile.

"So very, very slow," he murmured to himself, staring down the slopes. It had taken them nearly six hours to find the body. The daughter had arrived home from school, stepping off the yellow bus and skipping up the long driveway.

He'd watched her from the trees.

She'd entered the code that allowed her into the house. She'd called for her mother. He'd heard this—as at the time, he'd still been in the backyard.

Watching was a part of the fun.

How hard was it for these folk, in their enormous homes, with their seven figure bank accounts?

He chose the women specifically. Their mansions, their manors, their estates all faced the forest. The windows blinking like eyes under the sun.

They thought they owned these slopes. The mist, the trees, the mountains.

But the mountain served as his perch. He glanced towards the small pile of energy drinks scattered across the ground beneath the rock. He didn't believe in littering—certainly not in the woods. But the bottles were markers.

Reminders.

Nearly thirty of them, amidst the pine needles and wedged against mossy stones.

He'd come here week after week, watching with his binoculars.

Many of the windows *didn't* have blinds or curtains. The mountains weren't inhabited, and they didn't wish to obstruct the view.

Natural light the real estate agents called it.

To him, though, the windows were far more interesting than television screens.

People did unusual things when they didn't think others were watching. He pressed the binoculars to his face, watching where the police moved about the backyard. A man was standing in the second-story window, grim-faced, his usually neat hair accepting the furtive ministrations of scrubbing fingers.

The little girl had been sent away, picked up by a friend's mother.

The police moved about the yard, calling to each other. Now, at this distance, he couldn't hear much save the muffled voices. But he saw everything.

They'd found the body, buried where he'd left it. But they hadn't found the box—this was the curious part. At least not yet. They hadn't dug any deeper. Eventually, he imagined they would.

But for the moment, they were combing through the trees in the woods around the house.

He watched them, amused.

The third burial in the last three days.

And he was only getting started.

He glanced at the bottles scattered across the ground.

Each one signified a week up here. Thirty in total...

One week for each intended body. Thirty was the goal.

Eventually, he'd have to shift to a new location. But he was only just getting started. Strands of moss tumbled as he readjusted his position and swiveled his gaze, binoculars still raised. He peered down towards a new home.

Children playing in the family swimming pool. Splashing, laughing, slapping each other with pool noodles. Little Donnie, young Rosa, and sixteen-year-old Amber. He knew them by name. Knew when they went to bed. When they woke up. Knew which of them liked their father and which preferred their mother. He knew that Rosa hated peanut butter and jelly. Knew that Amber was sneaking out before midnight, using the trellis behind her bedroom window. Once, she'd even snuck a boy in.

He knew so much about the denizens of the affluent section of Pinelake.

His binoculars shifted again, landing on the largest house. Pure, gray stone. With a two-story Redwood patio. Ms. Ortega was sunbathing on the deck. Unaware of the crime scene two doors down. Or perhaps simply indifferent.

Evening was quickly approaching, now, the sun finally fading. But Ms. Ortega sat there in her bathrobe, flipping through a small novel, and occasionally taking a sip from the wine glass at her side. The bottle was half empty now.

She lived alone in that large home of hers. She'd gotten it in the divorce. Mr. Ortega had been unfaithful. But, what no one knew, no one except for *him,* Ms. Ortega had *also* been seeing someone. That had ended last week, though. And so now, twice brokenhearted, Ortega was drinking away her pain.

He zoomed in with the binoculars, studying the woman. He'd watched her for weeks, fascinated by her every movement. She was wearing that necklace she loved so much.

A diamond necklace. A very expensive one.

He swallowed, slowly licking his lips. Just then, something flashed by out of the corner of his eye. He frowned, readjusting and raising the binoculars once more to watch the crime scene.

A new vehicle—a sedan with tinted windows was pulling up. He stared, frowning as figures began to emerge.

Feds, by the look of them. He thought he recognized the tall man with the scarred hand.

But her?

The pretty, pale-faced woman with the dark hair... he hadn't seen her around...

He leaned in, the faint odor of moss and mist lingering on the air. "So why the hell do I recognize you?" he murmured softly. "Who..."

He trailed off, and then his eyes widened. He stared as she moved down the long driveway, nervously biting her lip and tugging at her long sleeves with each step. She wore far more *modest* clothing than Ms. Ortega did.

There wasn't much Ortega hadn't shared with her woodland watchers.

This woman, though...

She was frowning, glancing around as she moved, her eyes shifting. Something was off with her eyes, but he couldn't quite make out what from this distance.

As she walked though...

It suddenly struck him.

He knew her face.

She'd once lived in this town.

He knew *everyone* that lived in his town. He'd been watching for a very, very long time. But she hadn't lived in a wealthy part of Pinelake. No... no she'd lived with...

He went completely still, the pieces falling fully into place.

The Ghostkiller's daughter had returned to Pinelake. Just as he'd been told she would.

Now *that* was very interesting. Last he'd heard, she was some sort of badminton player... or something. One of those sports no one really watched.

He chuckled to himself, a low, rasping sound. He adjusted his grip on the binoculars, holding them up with his off-hand.

He wasn't sure what Artemis Blythe was doing back in Pinelake. He'd never hated her like so many others had. He had an assignment where she was concerned... eventually.

But for now, she wasn't the object of interest.

Not tonight.

No...

He shifted his binoculars back to the sunbather reading that book, sipping that wine, reclining on that Redwood porch.

Yes... yes, he knew what had to come next.

And this time, they would be investigating a crime scene two doors down.

How scrumptious. He smirked.

The women always seemed to think he was after one of two things. Their bodies or their jewelry.

But that wasn't it at all.

No... no, he wanted something far, far more delectable. Their fear was simply an appetizer. Their terror, a starter course.

Their death just the desert.

No... what came in between? That was what he wanted most.

Three down. Far, far more to go.

He was only just getting started.

5

Artemis shifted uncomfortably as she emerged from the back seat of the sedan. She took a couple of hesitant steps up a driveway scattered with pine needles.

The beautiful home was as large as she remembered. The redbrick structure boasted a turret with a black-shingled roof. The main entrance was ornamented by large, onyx-hued double doors. The garden, as always, was immaculate. Flowers of various kinds shivered in the evening breeze, amidst the garden beds.

Her eyes traced the windows facing the street. The blinds were closed, the curtains drawn. She thought she glimpsed faint movement on the second floor. A shift of shadow across a beam of light. But then this faded too.

Pine needles scattered as she took a few steps down the long driveway, moving around the side of the house.

As she moved, she felt a prickle along her spine. A slow, rising sense of discomfort. What was she doing here, anyway?

This place wasn't for her, was it?

The people here didn't want her. She ducked her head as she moved, trying not to present a silhouette to any neighbors that might be watching.

The FBI was one thing, but local officers would also be helping on the case. And the cops, at least fifteen years ago, had all been hired from the town.

She let out a faint, huffing breath. The knot in her stomach was still tightening. An icy fist somewhere near her navel. She tried breathing exercises, slow inhales, followed by a held breath, then a longer exhale.

But it didn't seem to work.

As she moved down the driveway, the mountains beyond caught her eye.

One thing could be said for Pinelake—it was gorgeous.

A low wreath of mist shifted through the prickling boughs and branches. Deep green gave way to dark browns. The woods covered the slopes, providing the gray stone and muddy outcrops with some sense of decency. The mountains watched just as much as the denizens of the town looked at the mountains.

In a staring contest, Artemis had little doubt who'd eventually win.

She inhaled the fragrant, forest air. Thanks to the nearby lake, after which the town was named, the breeze often smelled of petrichor, like a forest after a recent rainstorm. Clouds flitted in faint wisps across the sky, teasing the receding sun as it disappeared beyond the mountains.

"You really think you can find something we didn't?" a voice said at her side.

She glanced over.

Agent Forester was striding next to her, moving slower than his long legs might have allowed. Or perhaps the easygoing pace was like the rest of him. She wasn't sure if she found him irritating or amusing yet.

Perhaps *most* annoying, he didn't seem to care either way. He just kept talking.

"I mean, I get that you're a whiz or something, but damn... That takes some balls. Not that I think you have balls." He shot her a look. "You don't, do you?"

She sighed, moving along the side of the house, past a two-car, off-set garage and stepping around the back of the house. The asphalt was new. The outbuilding also new. But she remembered the basketball hoop Jamie had so loved. She also remembered a couple of the scuff marks on the red stone, where Tommy had practiced shooting small action figures with his pellet gun.

"I'll see what I can find," she said softly.

"And if not," he replied. "You really going to speak with your old man in prison? You don't seem to like the guy much. I read a bit of your case." He shook his head, wincing.

She shot him a sidelong look. "You know, you're not half as charming as you think you are."

"Half of exceptional is still twice as good as shit-all," he said without missing a beat. Again, he didn't sound offended.

She frowned but then went still as she rounded the back of the brick mansion.

Men and women in dark blue were moving through the backyard, pausing every now and then to take photos, or pick up small scraps and pieces of trash to place them in plastic bags. Occasionally, someone lowered a yellow plastic marker with a number on it, pointing something out. She counted at least fifteen figures moving about.

Artemis' gaze moved quickly around the scene, cataloging, considering. Mostly just watching to start.

The figures furthest from the screen door were the most relaxed. Their eyes only vaguely lingering on the branches and ground cover. Their motions lackadaisical.

The ones closer to the screen-door had more stilted, jittery motions. In part, she supposed this was due to the police sergeant standing near a large, toppled, flat-bottomed, black grill.

But also the large hole next to the toppled, rectangular grill was the source of much attention.

"Is that where she was killed?"

"Yeah—you looked through the file, right?"

She shook her head. She'd been texted a file in the car but had wanted to wait until she saw the scene herself. Another rule her sister had taught her.

Preparation for long form. Improvisation for blitz.

Artemis didn't have hours. She'd been given *one* hour to find something. One hour to come up with a lead the FBI had missed, or she'd given her word to go speak with a demon behind bars.

This wasn't an option.

Already, though, she could feel eyes flickering towards her. One drawback of her somewhat unique appearance was that people often recognized her. In the chess community it hadn't mattered.

But now, she could feel some of the local cops traipsing through the woods pause to stare. A few of them began whispering to each other. Sergeant Larry Dawkins, who'd had darker hair and a less bushy mustache fifteen years ago, was staring at her outright.

"Forester?" the Sergeant called, his tone tentative.

"What's up, bud?" Forester called back.

"Why... do..." Sergeant Dawkins tugged at his hat, shifting it uncomfortably. "Could I speak with you for a second?"

Forester hesitated, glancing towards the man, then back towards Artemis. As much as he seemed to enjoy playing the jester, he had a shrewd look in his eyes as he glanced around the crime scene. He cleared his throat slowly, then called out, in a far deeper, less jovial tone, "This is our new consultant. She'll be aiding on the case. We expect everyone to give her what she needs. Now, back to counting pine needles. Or whatever you lot were doing."

Artemis stared at the ground as he spoke. It wasn't like people hadn't already been staring.

As he finished, though, with an air of reluctance, the locals continued their work. A few of the feds who she didn't recognize shot her a cursory glance but then returned to their business.

Sergeant Dawkins was marching over to them now, though. His face turning red as he approached, his big, drooping, white mustache quivering in indignation. The man had a bit of a belly. This plus his mustache reminded Artemis of a walrus. His waddle and wide eyes didn't help.

"Forester," the Sergeant snapped. "Do you know who this is?"

He kept his voice low but not *very* low. Occasional glances and whispers continued to abound.

She sighed, ignoring this now. Her eyes were on the toppled grill and the open hole in the ground. The body had long since been moved.

Forester nodded. "Cute, isn't she?"

Artemis, who was beginning to understand Agent Wade's stoic nature in the face of his partner's personality, ignored the comment, scanning the ground.

"No," snapped the sergeant, his voice fierce. He was speaking as if she wasn't standing right there. "This is... She's a Blythe."

Forester nodded once. "Thank you."

"No. You don't get it. She's... Look, can I talk to you over here—wait, is Grant in the car? I think I see her in the car. Agent Grant!"

"Hang on, now," Forester said quickly. "Grant's making some calls. Look, don't worry about Ms. Blythe, alright?"

"You don't know who she is."

"I do, in fact. Well, not intimately. Not personally. Though, that I'm sure can change." He didn't say it to be coy. In fact, his tone didn't even change. As if somehow he were simply declaring his stream of thought.

She wasn't sure where his sociopathy started or where it bled into outright harassment.

For now, though, he was serving as a bit of lightning rod for the police sergeant.

So she slipped past the two men. She took a moment to glance back at the silver skeleton watch on Forester's wrist. She took a mental picture. One hour. That's how long she had.

In one hour, she had to come up with *something*.

She approached the hole, frowning at it.

Her attention zeroed in. Her focus narrowed. Tunnel-vision, some called it.

But this was a *disciplined* focus. As a child, when she'd gone to some of the shows her father held, she'd been trained to pick out *one* person in the audience. Only one. Read one at a time... that's what her old man had often said.

As much as she loathed him, many of the tricks and tips she'd picked up at his shows had come in useful over the years.

This, coupled with her sister's training had turned Artemis into the woman she was today.

Now, as she stared at the ground, she thought of it as an audience member.

Not an eager, easy-to-fleece sheep. But a bored, cynical member of the audience. These ones had always been her father's favorite to deceive.

A personal challenge.

She moved a bit, shifting around the hole. She spotted the gouge marks in the dirt. Spotted where red stained against the mud. The body had been placed in the ground. Her eyes moved to the grill.

It had been knocked on its side... But judging by the scrape marks in the mud, it had been moved...

She traced the marks with her fingers, moving them in front of her eyes.

And then she realized.

The grill had been placed on *top* of the hole.

To hide the body?

She shifted...

No.

Far worse.

The marks in the mud. The disheveled earth, the cracks along the side of the hole.

He'd buried Mrs. Kramer alive. He'd trapped her in the hole, covered her in dirt, judging by the shovel placed *on top* of the grill. Then placed the grill over the buried woman so she couldn't escape.

She must have been unconscious at the time, Artemis reasoned.

Another faint chill crept along her spine at this consideration. She moved slowly around the back of the grill, frowning into the mud. A faint stain of red... Had she been bleeding?

Only now, allowing herself an unfiltered first impression, did she pull out her phone, scrolling to the crime scene photos she'd been allowed.

It was a redacted file. Specifically given with most of the text and half the images blurred. For consultant's eyes only...

She didn't *want* to see those images. Didn't want to imagine Mrs. Kramer in such a state.

But she needed as much information as she could find. If she was going to catch the monster who'd done this, she needed to come armed with knowledge.

And so she scanned quickly through the photos.

The preliminary coroner's findings matched her initial assessment. Mrs. Kramer had been knocked unconscious by a blunt object. The back handle of a knife was the coroner's guess. She'd then been placed in the hole. Dirt had been piled on top. The grill then placed over the hole...

Something else, Artemis noticed.

The poor woman had been buried face-down. That way, if she ever woke, she wouldn't have known which way was up. Even if she had started digging, unable to breath, suffocating, she might easily have crawled in the wrong direction.

Artemis shifted uncomfortably, scanning through the rest of the report. She moved her weight from one foot to the next, frowning as she did.

Her eyes moved along the crime scene photos.

Slowly, she called out, "Forester."

"What's up, bud?" came the reply.

She frowned. "Please don't call me that." She tapped a finger against one of the photos. "Where's her wedding ring?"

Cameron Forester came to a halt at her side, the tall agent peering down at the image on the screen. "Huh," he said. "Maybe she took it off?"

"No," Artemis replied. "She never took it off."

"Didn't you say it had been more than a decade? People change, Ms. Blythe."

Another sigh. "I think I preferred, bud. Can you just call me Artemis, please?"

The handsome man ran a hand through his unkempt hair. He shrugged. "Suit yourself. So where's the ring?"

"Killer took it?" Artemis guessed. "Was there burglary in the other crimes?"

"No, not that we saw. The first victim was found at the bottom of a lake. She'd been swimming. All her clothing and jewelry and purse were left on the dock in a neat pile."

Artemis shivered at the description. "Who found her?"

Forester sighed. "Fisherman. A buoy was tied to her ankle."

"So... he wanted you to find her?"

"Looks like."

"And what about the second victim?"

"Burned in her car."

"Shit."

Forester nodded, his expression grim. "That time we *did* find jewelry. A ring and a necklace in the backseat."

Artemis paused now, frowning. Information had patterns if someone was willing to look long enough.

"In the backseat?" she said slowly.

"That's right."

"So... why was her ring in the backseat?"

"I... I dunno." Forester hesitated. "Huh. Good point."

Artemis glanced towards the hole in the ground, her brow furrowing deeper. Then, she said, "Did anyone find the ring? Searching in the woods? In the lawn?"

Forester shook his head. "Nothing found yet. The killer is careful. We might not even have connected all three murders. But they're all wealthy women over the age of twenty, killed in a ten mile radius. Plus, they're always found in the evening; coroner tends to put time of death around five pm."

"Why five?"

Forester shook his head.

She glanced at his skeleton watch. Only forty minutes left.

Why had the killer placed a ring and a necklace in the backseat of a car he'd set on fire?

And why had he taken the wedding ring from Mrs. Kramer but not the other victims? He'd left their jewelry...

Unless...

He'd also left Mrs. Kramer's.

Removed it... but left it.

She stared at the grass. "You're sure no one found anything?"

"Pretty damn sure."

"Huh. That shovel—have you already gotten what you need from it?"

"I suppose so. You want the shovel?"

"Yes, please."

Forester, to his credit, didn't erect many obstacles. With a shrug, he snatched the shovel off the toppled grill and handed it to her.

First thing first. She checked the grill. Using the shovel to lift the lid and glancing inside. Nothing. It hadn't been used in a while. She scanned the grass, looking along the ground.

Still nothing.

So if not removed... only moved...

Then...

She dropped into the hole, pushing the shovel into the dirt.

Physical effort wasn't exactly her realm of expertise. Her brother had once told her, quite seriously, that she had the muscles of a thinker. Still, she tried to keep in shape and often went for morning runs. A physical regime was part of success in her field.

Now, she shifted some of the dirt. It took her a few shovels, casting red earth across the grass, but then Forester said, "Hang on. Look at that."

She stopped. There, in the heap of material in her shovel, was a small piece of...

She leaned in, frowning.

Forester lifted it, dusting it off and staring.

"This look like the ring she's missing?"

Artemis nodded slowly. She recognized the diamond. The two emeralds set on either side. An expensive ring. Much like most of the house. But the killer hadn't taken it.

He'd left a necklace and a ring in the back of the second victim's car. Left the jewelry and wallet with the clothing of the first victim...

Patterns.

So what if...

She let Forester examine the ring and dug deep again. She pulled nothing but dirt. Another shovel. This time she paused... no, just a rock.

Another scoop of—

Thunk.

She went suddenly still, staring into the hole.

"What was that?" Forester said, still holding the ring but leaning in now.

Artemis gouged at the ground with the shovel, feeling the rough wood against her fingers. And then, she dropped to a knee and tugged.

A long, rectangular box was removed from the ground. She lifted it slowly, frowning. It was *very* heavy. She grunted, arms straining as she lifted. Large, flashy letters adorned the surface, reading *Charmen's.*

"What's *Charmen's?*" Artemis murmured.

"Beats me… that was just in there?"

She nodded, feeling a flush of excitement. She winced, heaving with a faint gasp and placing the box on the edge of the hole.

"Damn. Good work, bud."

"Please, stop."

"Here, let me see."

She lifted the box, placing it on the ground. And then, slowly, Forester opened the lid. The two of them stared into the container, and both went very still.

Small gold bars were arranged in stacks. There had to be twenty of the gold bars. Each of them about the size of a phone.

Forester whistled. "Huh. We might not have to check with your old man after all."

Artemis just stared at the gold. Her mind was spinning again. The killer had left a wedding ring in the hole. He'd buried Mrs. Kramer *right* on top of the gold.

He had known it was there.

Or else she'd told him.

But why would she have told him, unless he'd asked?

Artemis tapped her fingers against the shovel. She dug a bit more, but no other surprise items materialized.

As she stepped slowly from the hole, though, a voice suddenly snapped.

"What the hell do you think you're doing?"

There was the sound of thumping footsteps, a slamming door. Artemis glanced sharply over, and Forester turned away from the heavy box of gold.

"Hang on," Forester said quickly, holding up a hand. "Please hang back. Hey—hey, I said hang back!"

But an angry, young man was marching forward, his eyes flashing furiously, a finger jutting towards Forester. "That box has *nothing* to do with my mother's death. It's a family investment. Get the hell away from it."

6

Forester kept his arms outstretched in a placating posture. But Artemis noticed the tall man shift nearly imperceptibly. Dropping his weight onto his back foot, his arms still spread. Her eyes flicked to his cauliflower ear and down to one hand which had surreptitiously formed a fist.

Gone was Forester's teasing or easy-going prattle. Now, he tensed, facing the figure marching forward.

"I said hang back, man," Forester said firmly. "Please," he added.

But the young man kept marching forward. He shoved past Forester, snatching at the box. "That's ours!" he snapped. "You have *no* right!"

"I said hang back!" Forester warned again, a growl creeping into his voice.

"And who's this?" The man demanded. "Why in—hey!"

It happened so quick, Artemis would have missed it if she'd blinked. One moment, the irate man—wearing a charcoal gray business suit—had been steamrolling towards them, stooping into the dirt to close the lid on the box of gold.

The next, he hit the ground with a loud *whooshing* sound as air exploded from his lips.

Forester shook out his wrist, wincing as he did. "I didn't mean for things to go that way, bud," he said towards the man in the grass.

The strange maneuver had required Forester's leg and a quick yank of his right hand. Artemis blinked, trying to figure out exactly what had happened.

The man on the ground, though, was groaning, pushing into a sitting position. He glared daggers at Forester. "You just assaulted me in my own home!" he yelled.

"No," Forester said slowly. "I stopped you from tampering with evidence at a crime scene. I didn't hurt you, either." Then, with a shrug, he added. "Maybe you should head back inside."

The man on the grass frowned, pushing back to his feet and dusting himself off. Dust and strands of grass fluttered beneath his brushing fingers. He frowned at Forester, bit his lip, and—still glaring—said, "That gold has nothing to do with the murder. You don't have permission to take it."

Forester shrugged once. "If I'm honest, that's not my call. But it is evidence, and so we are going to have to hang onto it for a bit. How come you have gold buried in your backyard, sir?"

But the man was no longer paying attention. His gaze had darted towards Artemis. His eyes suddenly widened.

She blinked back at him, brushing a strand of hair behind her ear, pushing it back into the band of her ponytail. And then recognition dawned.

"Jamie?" she said slowly, frowning once.

He was tanner than she remembered him. His dark eyes set in an olive complexion—his father's influence. He had a square jaw, though not *too* square. His features were arranged just on the pretty side of masculine, with long lashes, sharp cheekbones and...

She remembered those lips.

Artemis felt a flush in her cheeks, standing next to a muddy hole, facing the boy who'd been her first kiss... Though he wasn't a boy anymore.

His business suit fit him well enough. The anger that had twisted his features was now slowly flitting away. He stared at her and then murmured, "Dear God, Artemis? Is that you?"

In that moment, she could have hugged him.

No fear, no anger, no hatred in his voice. If anything, he sounded glad to see her. The first and only person in Pinelake who wasn't scared of the Blythe family. Mostly, though, he just sounded surprised. "Are you... you're not FBI now, are you?" he said, stunned.

She shifted uncomfortably. Jamie's eyes darted back towards the muddy hole. His expression soured once more. He let out a long, shaking sigh. He stared at the ground for a moment, forgetting Artemis briefly. Forgetting the gold as well.

He swallowed and forcefully looked away, refusing to stare at the hole.

"That..." he trailed off, and she didn't know what he'd been about to say.

"Look, maybe you should head inside," Forester advised again.

Jamie puffed another breath. "That's our family's," he said, firmly pointing at the gold. "I'll expect every ounce accounted for. I know exactly what's in there. Do you understand?"

Forester shrugged once. "I'll try to steal only a little."

Artemis winced, resisting the urge to elbow the lanky agent.

Jamie glared, but then deciding the man was joking, he shot a final look towards Artemis. Equal parts stunned and in pain and furious. He said, quietly, "It's... it's *really* good to see you. I... I wish could stay and..." he shook his head, trailing off. He winced. "I'm really sorry. I should head back inside. I'm supposed to pick up Sophie."

Artemis didn't know who *Sophie* was. A girlfriend?

She felt a strange jolt of envy.

This wouldn't do, though. She hadn't seen Jamie in fifteen years.

Then again, she hadn't *dated* anyone in fifteen either. Her schedule, her routine, took up too much time. In fact, standing here by the hole, she'd already missed an hour review with one of her online message boards.

She sighed, giving a faint fluttering wave of her fingers as Jamie marched back away, shooting occasional looks towards Forester, glaring at the tall martial artist. As he hastened back into the house, pulling a phone from his pocket, Forester said, "Damn. I know that look, that fast draw on the phone. He's calling a lawyer."

"Well, you *did* hit him," Artemis said.

"I did *not.* I gently tripped him when he started touching evidence. We haven't dusted these."

"Look, your lawsuits are none of my business. Now, *that's* a lead," she said firmly, pointing at the gold. "It counts."

Forester nodded. "It counts. Grant's gonna be thrilled. Wade, too. Though, he doesn't show much emotion."

"My point," she said, "is that I found you a lead. So any hope of having me speak to—"

"That," he said quickly, "Is not my call." He stared back at the gold. "Why do you think this was buried back here? Clearly the son knew. He knew you, too."

"Everyone around here knows each other," she said defensively.

"Ah, I get it. There's a history."

"No. No, what? There's no history. Look, I don't know why there was gold back here. But one thing's certain: the killer knew it was here and left it."

"How do you figure that?"

"What are the chances that he dug in the *exact* spot where the gold was buried, hmm?"

Forester shook his head. "Low."

"Very low. So he knew it was there. Which is *very* bad news."

"And how do you figure *that*?"

"Because," Artemis said slowly, frowning at Forester. "He's not interested in money. Otherwise he would've taken the gold. Would have taken the jewelry from the other victims."

"I see."

"And if he's not interested in money," she said firmly, "then it means he's killing for some other reason. Someone who kills to steal is easy to find. Easy to understand. But..."

"But what?"

"It's a game to him. He buried her *on top* of the gold. It's funny to him. People who kill for *fun* those are the ones you need to watch out for."

Her mind went back to a man in handcuffs, a social services worker. The flash of police lights across the deck. She shivered, biting her lip and inhaling shakily. She glanced towards the door Jamie had passed back through.

She could still feel the way some of the local police were watching her, frowning when they didn't think Forester was watching.

She hadn't missed Pinelake.

Hadn't missed any of this.

Part of her wanted to simply call it good. She'd found something for the FBI. Now all she wanted was to get back on a plane, return to Salinas, sit in her small, cramped apartment, and study opening theory. By now the pundits and the players alike had already analyzed her game with Stefan Wright from a million different angles.

Improvisation was good. Improvisation with preparation was better. The order depended on the task.

She wanted to go home.

But standing there, staring at the box of gold, she couldn't help the questions now sifting through her mind.

Jamie was as good-looking as she remembered. It wasn't a very *impressive* look to be thrown to the ground. But he'd recovered his composure quickly enough; besides, his mother had just died.

This, though, she supposed was what bothered her most.

Jamie had seemed more concerned about the gold than his mother's death. Why?

Why had he stayed inside *until* the gold had been discovered?

She paused, then murmured. "Did anyone in the family mention anything about what was buried there?"

Forester shook his head. He was glancing past her now, and she followed his gaze to see Agent Grant and Agent Wade now emerging around the side of the house. The phone calls, apparently, had finished.

"Why not?" Artemis said quietly. "Why wouldn't they tell you? It seems like an important piece of information, no?"

Forester scratched at his chin, his eyes flashing. Though he had some odd tendencies, she could see the intelligence in those eyes. He said simply, "Unless they didn't want us to know it was there... One might think they were more concerned about hiding gold than helping us find their mother's killer..."

Artemis bit her lip.

This was *exactly* what she'd been thinking. Her eyes moved back towards a shattered screen door. A large cardboard box had been erected inside the house. But on either side of the cardboard, she spotted movement. Figures and silhouettes shifting about the house. She also spotted the study window, open. Furniture was toppled inside. The place overturned, pillows on top of desks. A cabinet pulled to the ground.

What was going on in Pinelake?

Three women dead? One drowned, one burned, and one buried alive ... Their jewelry, their valuables, left at the scenes of the crime. The first victim, Mrs. Burrows had been a neighbor. Her possessions hadn't been touched—left folded and placed neatly on the expensive boat: her clothing, a necklace, a small paperback of *The Invisible Man,* and her wallet. All of it had been mentioned in the redacted file she'd been given. But it pointed to one thing.

Someone was killing for fun.

And they weren't about to stop.

She let out a faint sigh. It wasn't going to *kill* her if she stayed a bit longer. Just in case she could offer some help. At least, she *hoped* it wouldn't kill her.

Agent Grant and Wade were now approaching, gesturing towards Forester. The tall kickboxer was pointing towards the gold now. He said something, but she wasn't paying attention.

Her eyes moved towards the mountains, watching the mist crown the peaks. Watching the green slopes rise to meet the night. Like sentries in the backyard, keeping watch on the large homes speckled through the valley.

As a child, she'd loved those mountains. Artemis and her brother and sister had spent hours wandering the slopes.

Now, though, even familiar stomping grounds made her feel...

Like a stranger.

Or worse.

Like a Blythe. The worst type of predator.

She could only hope to avoid a hunter's bullet.

7

AGENT GRANT HAD ASKED her to join, but Artemis was having second thoughts. She stood in the cold hallway, facing the interrogation room door, wincing as she shifted side to side. Nothing good would come of this. She could feel it in her bones.

This same station, eighteen years ago, had served as one of the most hated places she'd ever been forced to spend time in.

Hours and hours, day after day, week after week, they'd asked her about her father. They'd grilled her and Tommy, wondering how much they'd known about the Ghostkiller's activities. Wondering how on earth they hadn't seen or heard anything.

Tommy hadn't done much talking. He never had.

Artemis hadn't wanted to, but silence, she'd felt, would only be seen as an admission of guilt.

She had never stepped foot in a police station since. Especially not one so full of painful memories.

Forester was kicking a vending machine down the hall, jamming at some of the buttons and shaking his head as he tried to coax a granola bar to fall into the slot. She watched him briefly, her hand trailing against the cold knob of the door.

He looked over suddenly, frowning. When he spotted her, he waved towards the door. "Don't worry," he called, "Grant doesn't bite."

"I'm not worried about Grant."

"Oh. Wade? He *does* bite. Sit well clear."

She shook her head, somehow feeling a little *lighter* in the face of the humor. She let out a faint sigh. "I—I don't know what they think I'm going to offer."

Forester shrugged, shoving the vending machine a final time but then giving up with a sigh. "Beats me," he said. "Pull some more psychic magic like with the gold. That would help."

"I'm not psychic."

"Sure looked psychic to me."

"It wasn't..." She rubbed at the bridge of her nose. "I saw a pattern and took a shot. It might not have worked at all. But process of elimination suggested the ring was either in the killer's possession or in that hole. It wasn't in the grass. Wasn't in the grill. It *could* have been lost, but there were so many searchers it didn't seem likely."

"Look, just sit still, listen and try not to make anyone cry. You'll do great. Think of an interrogation like…" He paused, then snapped his fingers. "That checkers game of yours."

"Chess. It's a sport."

"No. No, it's not. I know sports. That's a game."

"Are you intentionally trying to be annoying?"

"Nope. Purely accidental. My point is, think of an interrogation as a chess game. The people on the other side of the table are your arch-enemies."

"Opponents."

"Their words are their playthings."

"Pieces."

"The louder they get, the angrier they are, the closer you are to crowning your king."

"You mean checkmate?"

"Exactly."

Artemis hesitated. She didn't want to admit it, but… in a way… as silly as it felt, this made *some* sense. Not that she'd ever tell Forester.

She nodded, flashed a quick thumbs up and then twisted the handle to the interrogation room, pushing the door open and stepping through.

The first thing she noticed was the chill temperature, as if the room were kept intentionally cold. Unpadded, metal seats circled a table bolted to the floor. There were no one-way windows in this room, how she'd imagined in her mind. Rather, four, blank, slab walls circled the space. A single, blinking red light flashed from a camera above the door.

And there, sitting behind the bolted table, her eyes landed on Jamie Kramer. Handsome as ever, and far less emotional now. His hands were folded on the chill, smooth surface. He still wore his business suit, and Artemis spotted a couple of grass stains on the sleeves where Forester had sent him tumbling.

And yet, now, Jamie was projecting an air of mustered dignity.

He sat nearly as straight-postured as Agent Grant, and his expression was almost as impassive as Wade's.

Grant and Wade sat across the table, both of them watching Jamie. Wade was taking notes in a small, yellow legal pad.

Grant was sitting still, cross-legged as ever, not a strand of pale hair out of place. Her emerald earrings caught the bright, fluorescent light from the tube bulbs in the ceiling.

"Ah, yes, Ms. Blythe," said Agent Grant, nodding politely and gesturing towards an empty seat. "I believe you two know each other, yes?"

Jamie shifted uncomfortably but shot her a quick look and a smile. Again, she couldn't help but notice the look in his eyes. No fear. No disdain. If anything, pleased to see her. In a town like Pinelake, she would have found pitiless indifference something of a respite.

To have open warmth was practically an oasis.

She slowly lowered into the metal chair, returning the awkward smile and nodding quickly. "Hello, again," she said softly.

"I—it's good to see you, Artemis. I'm sorry I didn't get to say a proper... well, given the circumstances..."

"No, it's quite alright. You have a lot on your mind." She winced but then hastily added. "I'm very sorry for your loss. I promise to help do what I can to find who did this."

Jamie's eyes darkened now. He frowned at the table, his fingers twitching. He swallowed once but then nodded. He had the look of a man attempting to keep quiet lest he reveal his emotions.

Artemis shot Grant a look. Unsettled, she realized both the agents were watching the two of them like hawks. More accurately, like vultures eyeing the jutting ribs in some emaciated prey. She inhaled slowly.

Sitting here, at a table, she was reminded of her first ever in-person tournament. The lights, the noise, the sweat, the constant tapping of her opponent's leg... It had all been so distracting. She'd lost her first game, in fact.

She'd come back to win the next ten.

But that first one had taught her a lesson.

Focus wasn't nearly so much about what she paid attention to. Rather, it was about what she ignored.

So she turned promptly away from the two agents. They wanted her in here. That was Grant's request.

So here she was.

And if they wanted her help, that was fine. But she didn't work for the FBI. She didn't work for any of them. Which meant she could do things her way. Whatever way that turned out to be, at least.

She ignored the agents, watching Jamie.

How often had she thought about meeting him again? He was even better than she remembered. And yet she'd glimpsed cracks in his normally stable nature. This, she decided, could certainly be forgiven. His mother had just been murdered, buried in their backyard.

But there were questions... Someone had killed her Aunt Donna. Her father was playing games with the FBI.

She'd already given her word to help.

And so, she went fishing. "Where did you get that gold?"

She didn't care about his response. People could lie. Their words often did. But non-verbals were harder to fake. Some people could do it. Her father had been a master of lying with both body and words.

But not Jamie Kramer.

She'd always liked this about him. Honest to a fault. Maybe that was why she liked her analysts, the Washingtons, so much. They were honest too... But Jamie's honesty had been something fifteen years ago. Time could change things.

As her question registered, she watched his posture. Watched the way he swallowed, Adam's apple bobbing. The way his fingers flicked towards the grass stain on his side. But he paused, his fingers half-hovering then returning to the table.

Something else she noticed.

He kept his hands close together and slightly angled.

The way they rested on the table wasn't natural...

She considered this for a moment but then realized what he was doing.

He was sitting as if his hands were cuffed.

They hadn't cuffed him. It wouldn't have gone well in a small town like Pinelake. The 5,000 members would very quickly have heard about the outsiders who'd dragged a victim's son off in handcuffs.

But though he wasn't cuffed, Jamie Kramer had clearly been arrested before.

Curious. He'd been such a boy scout growing up.

Only now, as she leaned back, having gleaned this piece of information, did she listen to what he was stammering.

"...trust the banks. We kept it in gold. A bit of mine, a bit of my parents'. Sophie's college fund is in there."

"And Sophie is?"

"Umm... My sister," he said slowly. "She's only nine."

Artemis blinked in surprise.

Jamie pointed, the motions of his hands still somewhat stilted. "That was my reaction when they told me," he said with a good-natured chuckle. But his amusement faded quickly again, and he frowned. "She was a gift. I—I don't know what she's going to do without mother."

Jamie sighed faintly. His sharp cheekbones stood out in the bright light. He passed a hand through the neat part in his hair and crossed his arms after, crinkling his business suit.

"I'm very sorry," Artemis said quietly.

She could picture the moonlit night in the woods. The sound of the Icicle River tumbling down the slopes. The scent of rain in the forest lingering on the air. She'd been crying, sitting on her favorite overlook, staring at the town below. One of the last times she remembered shedding tears. She'd just been able to spot the five-hundred acre lake after which the town had been named.

Mr. and Mrs. Kramer had forbidden them from wandering the woods at night, but it hadn't been a rule they'd enforced.

In the memory, Artemis could still recall the way tears had slipped down her cheeks. Could still remember her shoulders trembling. She remembered the way the moon had looked, winking over the canopy, casting coy and playful light, streaming through the branches to tinge the forest floor in hues of blue. In the night, deep in the dark forest, on the mountain slopes, Artemis Blythe had shed tears.

And then she heard the faint rustle. Movement through the forest.

She could remember the faint jolt of panic, the quick glance into the dark. And then, the slow, tingling sense of relief.

Jamie Kramer was standing awkwardly to the side, pretending as if he hadn't noticed her crying.

She could still remember what he said. "I think I lost something earlier," he had muttered.

Normally, Tommy had been with them in their hikes through the forest at night. But over the months, Jamie and Artemis had been spending more and more time together alone. Never for too long. Only quick moments captured around the house. A short conversation in an upstairs hall. A joke shared while cleaning dishes together. Jamie had volunteered more than once to help Artemis when it was her night to do the dishes. She had done the same.

She could still remember just how uncomfortable Jamie Kramer had looked. How red his cheeks had turned. Could still remember the way he had appeared standing in filtered moonlight, under rustling boughs. Jamie had been an athlete then, too. Well-built, confident. But in that moment, he had looked how Artemis felt.

"What did you lose?" She remembered asking. She had known he was lying. Even at the age of thirteen, she could still pick out people's intentions.

He shrugged. "A scarf." Then he winced with guilt and quickly said, "I'm sorry, I lied. I didn't lose anything."

Honest, eventually. That was how she had seen Jamie Kramer. His conscience always got the best of him.

In fact, spending time with Jamie had been one of the first influences to teach her to tell the truth. It wasn't like her father had impressed this value on their family.

Perhaps it was equal part Jamie's influence but also, watching her own father. How miserable his lies had made others. What he had done to them.

What he had done to their family.

Jamie Kramer had shaken his head. "I saw you coming up here. I, I was wondering if maybe," he trailed off, wincing. "I don't know. I think you're pretty," he had blurted out at last.

He hadn't been the first boy to tell her this. But he had been the first boy she wanted to hear it from.

Her cheeks had turned a similar hue to his. She remembered the way he had approached, pine needles crunching beneath tentative footsteps. He had been smiling when he thought she wasn't watching. She had smiled too.

That hadn't been the night they had kissed. But it had been the night she had fallen in love with Jamie Kramer. A young, inexperienced love. But the only time Artemis had ever fallen. In the fifteen years since, she'd never felt that way again. She couldn't say why it was so hard for her to conjure affection. More than one counselor and psychologist had tried to help her.

But all she knew was that night, on the mountain slopes, beneath the moon, in the dark forest, Jamie Kramer had sat next to her on an old, mossy log, talking well into the early hours of the morning. By the time they had realized how late it was, Artemis was no longer crying.

Jamie, somewhat awkwardly, had held her hand as they walked back down the slopes, towards the mansion.

Now, sitting in the interrogation room, it was impossible for Artemis to forget these memories.

Her cheeks prickled in the chill room. She studied the man across the table. Was he still honest, eventually?

Or had time ruined him, like it did so many?

Why had he seemed more concerned about the gold in the hole than his mother?

"Look," Jamie said, slowly, studying her expression. He wasn't trained by a cold reader. His father wasn't a mentalist. But Jamie had always been emotionally intelligent. He must have spotted the look in her eyes. "I'm very sorry for how I behaved back there. I wasn't trying t–I mean to say–just..." He trailed off, rubbing ruefully at the back of his head.

"You are under stress," she said simply.

He nodded quickly. "Exactly. Look, I'll admit, things haven't been the same at home. Not how you remember them. My mother," he sighed and trailed off, shaking his head. "She's been having a rough time recently. Some personal issues—drowning herself in wine and that pretentious book club of hers."

"What sort of personal issues?" Agent Grant cut in.

He shot her a look. "With my father," he said. "They were going to get a divorce. At least, they were talking about separating."

"You always were your father's son," Artemis said quietly. She could glimpse grief in his eyes but now also understood the strange coldness towards his mother's death. Jamie was loyal to a fault. If he chose to trust someone, he did it without hesitation. It had cost him in his friendship with Tommy more than once. And if his parents had been having marital issues, and he had chosen his father's side, then she could see how it would be difficult for him to navigate his emotions.

"Were you angry at her?" Artemis said.

"No," Jamie said quickly. But then he paused, sighed. Honest, eventually. "Yes. Yes, very. In fact, I was mad at her sometimes. Mad at what she was doing to my dad. To me. To Sophie. We had a good family growing up," he murmured, shaking his head. "If not for her, you and Tommy would still be in town."

Artemis frowned, wondering if she should say something. This was not what she remembered. The arguments she had heard had always involved Mr. Kramer pushing to have Tommy and Artemis kicked out. And when Tommy had run away, that had been the last straw.

But now wasn't about rehashing the past.

Agent Wade interjected now. He'd removed his sunglasses and had tucked them in the collar of his suit shirt. He stared with eyes like chips of flint across the table. His thickset shoulders and barrel chest only adding to the intimidating effect. "Can you think of anyone who might have wanted to hurt your mother?" Agent Wade said in that gruff, monotone voice of his.

"My mother was like most people in this town. She didn't have many enemies. Her comfort was her best friend."

Artemis shot Jamie a look. She glimpsed the disgust in his gaze.

"If no enemies, why bury that gold?" Wade said.

"I told you before. We have some money in the banks, some in stocks. But we diversified. It isn't a crime to own gold."

"No," said Wade, "but whoever killed your mother *knew* where that gold was. Can you think who might have done it?"

Jamie just shook his head. "No one knew..."

"Actually," Artemis interjected, clearing her throat uncomfortably, "they *didn't* know where the gold was."

All three sets of eyes turned towards her.

8

"How do you mean?" said Agent Grant.

Artemis winced under the glare of the bright, fluorescent light. Her hands felt clammy and cold, and she rubbed her palms under the table against her legs. But projecting what little confidence she'd summoned, she said, "The pictures from the coroner." She shot a quick look towards Jamie whose expression had gone stiff. "Umm... Mayb e... Maybe I should mention this later when—"

"No, go ahead," Jamie said firmly. "If this helps catch the bastard then don't stop on my account. I was there when they dug her damn corpse out of the ground. I had to hold my father while he wept. My old man's health has already been failing, and seeing her like that nearly killed him. Despite their marital difficulties, he still loved her. So go ahead. I want to find who did this just as much as you."

Artemis clasped her hands together, if only to grasp something solid. "Right. Well, in the coroner's photos, Mrs. Kramer had blisters on her fingers. She was the one who dug the hole."

"That doesn't mean the killer didn't know where the gold was," Grant pointed out.

"No... but the overturned study does."

Grant and Wade were frowning at her. But Jamie nodded suddenly, pointing at Artemis. "She's right," he exclaimed. "My mother worked from home. Someone tore through her study. It was a mess when we got home. If the killer knew where the gold was buried, why did he first look in the study?"

Artemis nodded. "A few possibilities. Obfuscation, misdirection, looking for something else." She shrugged. "But most likely, coupled with the callouses, the killer didn't know where the gold was. Which leaves one question."

Now, she returned her full attention to Jamie. She kept her voice firm. "Who *knew* about the gold but didn't know where it was buried?"

"The only people who *knew* where it was buried were my parents," said Jamie. "I didn't even know exactly. I knew it was somewhere on the house premises. But I didn't know until tonight when my father told me."

"So you didn't know the location of the gold?" Grant said.

"No one did," Jamie replied. "And the only person who knew we had it..." He trailed off, frowning. His eyes flicked towards Artemis, and he let out a faint sigh. "It was legal, mind you. Perfectly legal."

Wade said, "People don't usually lead with that."

"Say what you want," Jamie snapped. "I had a friend who knew a guy. This guy lived in Seattle."

Artemis frowned. "What *friend*?" she said, already dreading the answer.

He shot her an uncomfortable look. "Tommy," he said. "Tommy introduced me to a jeweler friend of his. He dabbled in gold sales."

Grant was glancing between the two of them now. "What's the matter?" she said, studying the look on Artemis' face. "Who is this Tommy?"

"My brother," Artemis replied primly. "He's connected to the Seattle mob. If he introduced your family to a jeweler, then whoever you bought that gold from has ties to the mob."

"And do you think your brother is involved?" Grant insisted.

"No," Artemis and Jamie both said at the same time.

Artemis shot Jamie a quick look of gratitude. But she was already rising from the metal chair. It was too uncomfortable on her back. Too cold on her legs. Nothing about this horrible place appealed to her. "No," Artemis said simply. "But this jeweler knew where the gold was. Which means the mob knew."

Jamie wrinkled his nose. His voice shook, "Do-do you think this is mob related?"

Artemis considered the question. Three victims already. All of them wealthy women. None of them had been robbed. They'd been killed in horrible ways. Someone was trying to send some sort of message. But on the other hand... whoever was killing was *enjoying* themselves.

"It's some psychopath," Artemis said simply. "I can't think of a better place to find one of those than organized crime. I don't know much, but if I were going to speak to someone, it would be this jeweler. Now—it's getting late. And I have to head back to my hotel. My flight is early tomorrow morn—"

"What if we paid you?" Grant said swiftly, cutting her off.

"Excuse me?"

"A consultant fee. What if we *paid* you?"

Artemis hesitated. "I... I don't need the money. Not anymore."

Grant sighed, massaging the bridge of her nose. "Forester was telling me where he remembered you from. You took part of the agency's preliminary recruitment test, yes?"

"A few years ago, that's right."

"Well, I looked at your marks."

Artemis frowned. Jamie glanced towards Grant. "She didn't miss a single question, did she?" Jamie murmured.

Grant shot him a look, her eyes flashing. She gave a quick shake of her head, her expression still severe. "No. In fact, she corrected one of the questions. It would be a one-off thing," Grant said. "Just until we find out what's going on in Pinelake. You have connections here, Artemis. You've proven..." she swallowed and folded her hands again, "somewhat *useful*."

Jamie was staring at the table now, lost in his own thoughts. Artemis felt stuck. She didn't want to refuse to help in front of Jamie. She'd already decided she wanted to put her father in his place. Wanted to help as best she could.

But to come on as a full consultant? She'd already found them a lead, hadn't she?

A jeweler for the mob, moonlighting as a psychopathic killer most likely.

Grant and Wade were both staring at her. Then, Grant said, "Of course, I understand if not. Wade, please make sure to bring this Tommy person in for questioning."

Artemis went stiff. "Wait, hang on. No—you heard Jamie. My brother has nothing to do with this."

Grant looked Artemis directly in the eyes. "If you were consulting, you'd have a say. But as you're leaving..."

Artemis scowled. She stood facing the older agent, meeting the woman's rigid features. Stiff-backed, stiffer upper lip, Grant didn't so much as blink in the face of Artemis' glare.

But Artemis had played tougher, more seasoned opponents before. So this was how the woman wanted to play it? She was so determined to solve the case, she was willing to threaten Artemis' brother?

One enemy at a time.

Artemis let out a faint sigh. "Do you really think strong-arming me is going to help?"

"Begging didn't work," Grant replied, her tone cold. "Bribery didn't work."

"Bluffing won't either."

"I'm not bluffing Artemis. There are three women dead and no sign that our killer is about to stop. We have a lead that *you* found for us. My job, Artemis, is *not* to be the smartest person in the room. It is to *find* the smartest people and utilize their skills. Is that clear?"

Grant was now standing as well, facing across the table, one hand braced against the metal as if preparing for a sudden wave on a ship.

Artemis met the woman's calculating gaze. Part of her admired Grant for it. A bold move. A strong move. But at least she was being honest.

On the other hand, Artemis *hated* being backed into a corner.

Zugzwang. That's what it was called in chess.

The moment before you knew you had no choice left.

She hadn't seen Tommy in years. But she couldn't let him get involved in this. Her brother did *not* play well with others. He had some... authority issues, to state it mildly. And over the last decade or so, she highly doubted any of this had improved.

Especially if he was introducing old friends to mob jewelers.

And on the other hand...

Her eyes flitted towards handsome Jamie Kramer. The only warmth in Pinelake. He'd been happy to see her. Even with his mother dead, his life in turmoil, everything collapsing. He'd still had enough time to spare her a smile and a nod.

Of course, she didn't think they could start things where they'd left them. Certainly not...

And Mrs. Kramer hadn't deserved to die like that. Artemis' father was playing everyone. So many moving pieces and motives.

This, she remembered distinctly, was why she'd refused to return to Pinelake.

"Well?" Grant said, firmly. "Do I arrest your brother, or do we have a new consultant?"

Jamie had perked up again, paying attention once more. "You're a bit of a bitch, you know that?" he said, scowling. "Artemis didn't do anything to you."

"Hey," Wade snapped. "Show some respect."

But Grant held out a calming hand to her pitbull. She ignored Jamie, ignored Wade. Her eyes fixed on Artemis. The Ghostkiller's daughter stood in the cold room, mulling over her options.

But then she let out a long sigh and shrugged. "Fine. I'll go speak to this jeweler."

"Good," Grant said, neither sounding pleased nor displeased. More like a computer, taking in information and moving onto the next step. Emotions didn't factor. "I'll send an agent with you for backup."

As the woman said it, Artemis couldn't help but feel as if she were a pawn in a queen's game. She didn't like feeling like a piece to be used.

But whatever was going on here, she felt certain she wasn't being told everything.

One enemy at a time. That's what Helen had said.

Then again, all of Helen's rules... her advice...

Had earned her an early grave.

Artemis bit her lip, shot Jamie a quick, apologetic look. "I'm very sorry," she whispered. "For everything."

And then she turned, stalking back out of the cold room.

9

Night had fallen, but the gloomy, dark atmosphere of the run-down section of Seattle didn't seem to bother Artemis' new partner in the least. No sign of the Space Needle, no glimpse of a bridge that looked as if it were floating. The charm was somewhat lost in this bare bones section of the rainy city.

But Forester was whistling cheerfully, guiding their vehicle through the dingy streets, alongside cracked sidewalks and beneath busted safety lights. Figures occasionally lingered on street corners, watching the vehicle with the tinted windows.

Artemis shifted uncomfortably under the scrutiny. It was like having gawkers in an autograph line after a game... Except in this case, the gawkers wore upturned hoods and had poorly concealed weapons jammed into their waistbands.

Artemis slouched in her seat as they rolled slowly past a couple of young men passing a brown paper bag through the window of a parked truck. She tried to melt into her seat, hoping to hide from view.

"Ah," Forester said cheerfully. "This should work." He came to a complete stop in the dark side-street, right next to the men with hidden weapons. He then rolled down the passenger-side window.

Artemis' window.

As the window lowered, Forester leaned across the seat, peering out.

The two men who'd been handing the item through the open window of the truck whirled around. Their hands darted to their waists. One of them glared from beneath his hood, panic flashing in his gaze. The truck behind them floored the gas, peeling away with a squeal and a trail of smoke.

"Hello, gentlemen!" Forester called out, adding a little wave of his scarred fingers. "Do either of you know where *Charmen's* jewelry store is?"

"Who the hell are you?" snapped one of the men.

"I'm happy to pay," Forester added.

Both of the men on the street corner went still. One of them was glancing curiously at Artemis. She slumped even further in her seat, wishing now that Grant had given her Wade as a babysitter instead.

"Forester," she whispered, through barely moving lips. "Let's get out of here. *Now.*"

A couple of other guys, from the direction the truck had gone, emerged from an alley and where now circling back around, returning to get a good look at the strange vehicle in their territory.

Artemis could feel a clot forming in her stomach again.

Forester, though, was now peeling hundred dollar bills from his wallet, waving them past Artemis. "I've got a bunch more where that came from," he said merrily. "But I'm afraid I can only give you a hundred a piece. So, *Charmen's?*"

"How much more you got?" asked one of the men.

Artemis wanted to reach over and kick the tall man.

Forester flashed a grin. There was something distinctly *lupine* about the expression though. He winked—actually *winked* to the men on the street corner. "I can get out and show you, if you like," he said conversationally. But now there was a quality to his voice that made Artemis perk up. Both the men were now paying attention also. The two approaching from the alley were moving slower now, frowning and watching.

One of the young men whispered something in the ear of his friend. The other hesitated, pointing at Forester. "Do I know you?"

Forester shrugged. "I guess I have one of those faces. So should I get out and show you my wallet, or will you take the two hundred and give me directions?"

Never once did the man with the lumpy left ear drop his smile.

But the two young men shifted uncomfortably, shot glances back towards their compatriots approaching up the street. One of them frowned at Artemis, and again she wished she could vanish into thin air.

But finally, one of the men slipped his hand from his waistband, tucking a glint of silver back under his sweatshirt.

"*Charmen's* is up that way. Two streets over. Place smells like fish. You can't miss it." He extended his hand.

And Forester handed the two, crisp hundred-dollar bills. But then, he pulled something else from his wallet. "Here," he said. "Another hundred as a thank you. Plus two business cards."

"Cards? What cards?"

"A boxing gym. I run it with some of my friends."

Suddenly, the two men on the street corner's expressions completely changed. White teeth flashed. Eyes widened in excitement. One of them even emitted a little squeak like a schoolgirl at a Justin Bieber concert. "Holy shit! I knew I recognized you! You're BamBam!"

Cameron Forester chuckled. "It's been a few years since I was called that."

"Holy..." The two men were now gesturing excitedly at their approaching compatriots. "Oi, Jer—shit come over. You won't believe who it is!"

The two other men, who'd been stalking forward, slowed a bit, hesitant. They were now clearly very confused.

Artemis didn't blame them. The sentiment was shared.

Forester was chuckling now, and handing out two more business cards. "First lesson is free," he said with a nod. "Come in any time. Tell them I sent you, and they'll give you my schedule so we can arrange something. It's nice to meet fans."

The one named Jer reached the car now, peering in. He was still frowning. "Who the hell is BamBam?" he asked.

Artemis wanted to add an *amen*.

"Cam 'BamBam' Forester," snapped the first man, who'd been grinning the widest. "Two time, two division MMA champion, boss. Who do you think?"

The second man at his side was wagging his head in enticement. "I remember that fight with Bonesy! He broke your arm!"

Cameron chuckled. "I remember that fight too."

"Yeah, but you gone and knocked him out anyway. Was some *crazy* shit, man. Real crazy. I got that poster and everything!"

Cameron flashed another full-tooth grin. This one wasn't nearly so feral or wolfish. It was strange how the man was able to do that. The same smile but two different meanings. This one was a playful, friendly look of amusement. The one from earlier had been barred teeth in a threat.

It was in the eyes, Artemis decided. Though she made a mental note to pay closer attention.

Jer frowned in suspicion. He hesitated. "You a celebrity or something?" he asked, peering into the car. Artemis was completely forgotten at this point. Though, she wished next time Forester would roll down his own damn window to talk to men on dark street corners.

"Nah," said Cameron. "Nothing like that. Artemis here, though, is a bit of an internet celebrity. She's a checkers player."

"Checkers? Shit—that's like, heady stuff, yeah?"

"That's right, Jer," Forester said. "Real heady. I'm sure she'd be happy to give her autograph if you—"

"Nah. Forget that man. Can we get a selfie?"

Artemis felt fairly certain *no* wasn't an answer she could give. She glared at Forester. But he just beamed back. "Here, I'll lean in too, if you like," Cameron said.

The four men now gathered around the window, reclining back, raising their phones. Artemis blinked as the lights flashed. Forester raised two thumbs up, grinning past Artemis where he leaned over the divide between the seats.

After another few photos, Forester called, "Alright. We gotta get. Good meeting you all. Don't forget—first lesson is free!"

The men all nodded, waving excitedly and comparing the pictures on their phones.

And then, mercifully, Forester finally pulled the vehicle forward along the side street and in the direction they'd been pointed.

As the tires crunched over old, worn roads, and they bumped over an actual entire bag of trash left in the middle of the street, Artemis furiously rolled up her window.

"Are you crazy?" she demanded.

He looked at her. "Isn't nice to make fun of someone's disability."

"Don't even start," she snapped. "I'm not making fun. And my issue is with your twisted sense of humor. You thought that was *funny!*"

The tall man hesitated, considering this. Then grinned. "Yeah. I guess I did. You were a champ, Checkers. You didn't miss a beat. Good on ya."

"It's chess. Not checkers. Which you know at this point but keep saying just to irritate me."

He was peering through the windshield now, clearly ignoring her, and watching the store fronts move slowly by. "You don't smell fish, do you?"

"I—what?"

"They said the place smells like... Ah, there—think that's it? There's a few stalls in that store next door. Maybe it's for halibut."

"Hang on, hang on," Artemis interjected, shaking her head firmly. "If I'm going to be partnering on this case—"

"Consulting," he corrected. "Not a partner. More like hired help."

"Fine. *Consulting. Helping.* Call it what you want. But we need some ground rules."

Forester pulled their vehicle alongside the curb, coming to a slow, grinding halt. He shot her a long look. "Alright. What rules?"

"No... none of *that* back there," she said. "I get it. You're a big tough man. Well, big tough man—don't put me in harm's way just to stroke your own ego!"

"That's what you think I was doing?" Forester said, frowning.

"Wasn't it? You took a selfie."

"They wanted that. But no, Ms. Blythe, *chess*master. A few hundred bucks allows those guys to go home early, meeting their quota without the risk of getting shot. Showing my face gives them something of a motive to check out that gym. We have more than six professionals and twelve full-time amateurs who were introduced to us... by business cards. If you know what I mean."

"I don't."

"Gangbangers, ex-cons, lowlifes, do-nothings. *My* people," he said firmly.

Artemis blinked. "You... you were *actually* trying to recruit for your gym?"

"Two birds with one stone, miss smarty pants. We found the jeweler's and I may have earned *BamBam's* some new clients."

"Your gym is called BamBam?"

"Mhmm."

"And *you* are called BamBam?"

"It's a nickname. All fighters get them. I'm sure you chess folk have nicknames too, don't you?"

"Well... online I have a username."

"Oh? What's that?"

Artemis sighed. "Artemisblythe01."

"Huh. Super creative."

"Hard to compete with BamBam."

Forester flashed a wink, and then pushed out onto the sidewalk. Artemis frowned after him. She wasn't sure what to make of Agent Cameron Forester. An ex-MMA champion now working as a federal agent. A sociopath according to his colleagues...

He was equal part chipper, playful and downright frightening.

She wasn't happy with the way he'd manhandled Jamie back at her old friend's parents' home. And that stunt back there? Forester got off on it. He enjoyed putting her in an uncomfortable position. That much was obvious. He wasn't *nearly* as charming as he thought he was.

She settled on this, grumbling to herself and scowling as she pushed out of the front seat and moved onto the sidewalk behind Forester.

As she did, and the door clicked shut behind her, she glanced at the skeleton watch, visible past Forester's sleeve.

Nearly Ten PM.

Well into the night. The streets were mostly clear, save the buzzing lights of a few strip clubs and bars visible further down the sidewalk. The faint scent of something pungent lingered on the air. *Not* fish... something stronger. She wrinkled her nose. "What *is* that?"

"Formaldehyde," Forester replied without hesitating. "Taxidermist. Second floor, see?"

He pointed, and her eyes moved up, spotting a window display with a large grizzly bear standing motionless, arms outstretched to embrace the glass.

She stared at the stuffed bear, feeling a strange prickle along her back.

"Not right, that," Forester muttered, shaking his head and staring at the bear. "Thing like that shouldn't be trapped and stuffed. Isn't right."

"Is that how you feel?" Artemis shot back. "Once the king of the jungle, now trapped and stuffed?"

Forester looked at her slowly. And she felt that same chill now spread across her arms. The twinkle was gone from his eye. The humor gone from his tone. "Hey, Ms. Blythe. One thing."

She swallowed.

"Don't psychoanalyze me, alright? You mentioned some rules. That's mine. Sound good?"

Again, she was reminded of a sort of lupine stare—a wolfish glare through the dark. The fangs weren't visible on Forester... not always. But he had them. She would have to remember that.

"Alright, fair," she said, swallowing. "And… and sorry."

He beamed now, shrugging. "No harm, no foul. And… yeah, sorry for scaring you back there. I wasn't trying to. Here—there's *Charmen's*. First floor. And looks like someone's home."

He began moving up the sidewalk towards another window display. A faint, yellow light was visible through the dark glass in the back of the store.

Artemis followed quickly, frowning as she did. "Is it true what they said back there?"

"About my good looks and sense of humor?"

"No. About breaking your arm…" She frowned. "That's not possible, is it? To break your arm but then still win the fight."

He shrugged. "I mean… not sure about possible. Just know that's how it happened." He had come to a stop in front of the glass door, his breath fogging the glass as he peered into the shop.

"So you got your arm broken… And then you… what?"

"Knocked the guy out with my other damn arm. Took like five minutes though. Painful shit. Still got the reminder in my elbow. Alright… I mean, someone is *definitely* moving around back there. Is this a doorbell?"

The lanky fighter pushed a thick thumb against a small, white button next to the front, glass door.

Artemis frowned, listening as a small bell echoed from inside the shop.

She'd also spotted the moving silhouette against the bright backdrop. The shadow went still at the sound, though.

Forester tried the bell again. The shadow began to move.

"Remember," Artemis whispered, "if my brother set this up, then whoever this jeweler is, he works for the mob."

"This brother of yours sounds like he could use some boxing lessons."

Artemis grimaced. "He's had those. He just..." she sighed. "He has authority issues."

"Don't we all. Mob, though. Got it. I've had some cases involving organized crime in the past. Not nice guys."

"No, not nice at all," Artemis said, remembering some of the news articles she'd seen online when first attempting to convince Tommy to get the hell away from his contacts in Seattle.

But her twin brother had never been much like Artemis. Strategy games and years doing the same thing, hours and hours a day, was his version of hell. Tommy was the type to rush into a situation before thinking about it. She could remember, once, when they'd been children, how Helen, Tommy and Artemis had gone fishing. They'd eventually decided to take a dip in the lake.

Looking up from the small, collapsible, wooden chess board, Artemis had eyed the lake hesitantly. She'd eventually summoned the courage to dip a toe in the water, testing it. Helen had *watched* Artemis and Tommy, gathering information from her siblings by proxy. Tommy hadn't hesitated. No sooner had the words, "Let's go swimmi—" left Helen's throat—following a clever series of moves on the wooden board in the bottom of the boat where she'd captured Artemis' rook—then Tommy had sprinted to the edge of their fishing boat, nearly toppled the thing and dove into the water with a shout.

He'd forgotten to take out the five dollar bill he'd stolen from the bait shop register—the money had been ruined. Along with his watch and a half-eaten pack of pretzels.

Now, though, Artemis wished she could channel a little bit of her brother. She shifted uncomfortably, watching as the figure approached through the glass. A late night rendezvous with known mob affiliates was *not* her brand of "fun."

More than anything, Artemis wanted to jump back in the car, roll up the windows and lock the doors.

Then again, if she did that, Forester would likely just roll the windows down again and point her out to some gun-totting thug.

Really. He was too much.

Now, though, she stayed her ground, standing next to her accompanying agent. Up until now, she hadn't *fully* appreciated his size. Six-foot-four *easy* if not six-five. He wasn't as broad-shouldered or barrel chested as Agent Wade, but he had a lanky strength about him.

She found herself taking a half step *back,* placing Forester directly between her and the jewelry shop's door.

The shadow now arrived at the door.

10

A FACE WITH A thick brow and a very neat, trimmed beard was staring out at them. The figure flashed a middle-finger and used the digit to tap at the closed sign.

Forester pressed the bell again.

"Don't antagonize him," she muttered beneath her breath.

He didn't hear. Or at least, pretended as if he didn't.

Instead, he waited patiently on the other side of the glass door, watching the figure within.

The man scowled out into the night, but she noticed his hand twitching where it trailed against the glass. A small, pink tongue darted out, wetting dry lips. He shot a nervous look past Forester towards where Artemis was hanging back.

She forced a quick smile. She'd intended to communicate comfort. Instead, she thought she'd projected constipation. She didn't even have a damn gun. She glanced towards Forester's hip. His own service weapon was hidden beneath the edge of his mis-buttoned jacket.

The large man tapped thick knuckles against the glass, then added a little finger-rolling wave.

The man on the other side of the glass hesitated a second longer... Now, his hand was straying to his hip.

"Don't do it," Forester muttered, still smiling. "Don't you do it..."

It took Artemis a second to realize he wasn't talking to her. She'd been distracted by the many glistening objects just visible past the two layers of security glass. The man had stepped through a sliding, metal curtain—which hadn't been closed yet, but if he wanted could be shut to seal off the entrance.

Past him, in rectangular, glass display cases, she spotted ornate cushions—mostly red or black or blue. The only light came from the open door at the back of the shop. And so it felt as if she were staring into a field of stars.

Small, winking, twinkling lights from the many ornate necklaces and rings and jewelry ornamenting the display cases.

Forester raised his voice. "Let's chat for a second, huh?"

The man on the other side of the glass had finally reached a decision. He seemed to decide these strangers were suspicious enough to warrant the next stage of caution.

His hand darted to his hip, reaching into his waistband. She glimpsed a flash of metal.

It was as if *everyone* on this block was armed.

But Forester moved faster. His weapon was in his hand, his badge in the other. The gun now tapped against the glass.

The man with the thick brow went still. He blinked owlishly, swallowing slowly, his eyes fixated on the gun.

Artemis muttered. "He didn't close the metal curtain."

"Yup." Forester whispered, his smile still fixed, his eyes still on the man inside the shop. "Doesn't look like he knows it's there, does it? He's an intern."

"A what?"

"Low-level gun thug. But also... our ticket in."

Forester tapped his muzzle against the glass, then tapped his badge. Then he nodded towards the lock. The man on the inside had frozen like a statue. His fingers trailing towards his own weapon. But now, slowly, his hand moved. With a glare, he reached towards the lock.

"There we go," Forester whispered. "That's it. Nice and easy. Open up, bud."

Click.

Forester moved fast, shouldering the door open *hard*. The frame slammed into the nose of the gun thug on the other side. The man was sent reeling with a faint shout. As Forester entered the jewelry shop, he stowed his badge, holstered his gun in the same, swift motion, and used a free hand to snatch at the reeling mobster.

The air held the faint fragrance of too much aftershave. From further back, in the direction of the yellow glow, Artemis heard the faint sounds of music emanating through the jewelry shop.

She watched, horrified as Forester's forearm looped around the mobster's neck. The man kicked, struggled, but then eventually went still.

"Did—did you kill him?"

"No, shh. Just don't want any surprises further in. I don't think they hear us—music's loud. Here, take this."

She gaped at the weapon extended towards her. "I... I don't want to."

"Take it, come on."

She shook her head. He rolled his eyes, disassembled the gun in a few quick motions, and sent the pieces scattering into various directions across the smooth, tiled floor. Then, pressing a finger against the unconscious man's neck, he nodded to himself and stood to his feet.

The tall man's large shadow stretched back, swallowing the threshold. He glanced at her, quirking an eyebrow. "You coming or just enjoying the view?"

"I... I..."

"You can sit in the car if you like," he murmured. "This guy *shouldn't* wake in time to see you. I'm sure he'll be very nice if he does—"

"Fine. I'm coming..." She gingerly avoided the unconscious gun-thug, stepping over him as she entered the jewelry store. "I hate you," she muttered beneath her breath.

"Thin line between love and hate, Checkers. Come on—let's see if we have any more friends in the back."

"What if that was the store owner?"

"Wasn't."

"How can you be sure?"

"Because," Forester whispered back, moving slowly into the store. "The glass is bulletproof."

She stared at the back of his head. "Excuse me?"

"The glass, Ms. Blythe. It's a jewelry store. It's bulletproof. My weapon wouldn't have done shit-all."

"I... you were bluffing?"

"Yup. Now hush, I think there's a few of them up ahead. You sure you don't want that piece?"

"The—the—"

"The gun, Checkers."

"No! No, I don't. Just... stand in front of me. You're big. Block bullets or something."

He snorted, shaking his head as he moved across the tiled ground. Artemis was severely regretting her decision to come. She hadn't wanted them to arrest her brother. In a way, this small favor was helping to alleviate the guilt she'd felt for not visiting... or calling... or writing...

Or being what a twin sister was supposed to be.

Now, though, she was beginning to wish she'd just purchased a post-card or something. All of this... it was too much. She was supposed to be back home, celebrating her victory. Analyzing the game...

But instead...

She swallowed.

She was walking into a mobster hangout with a loose cannon.

Suddenly, over the faint sound of music, she heard voices. Yelling. Her heart went still and her mouth went dry. She let out a little squeak and stared as another shadow appeared in the doorway at the back of the store.

11

As SHE STARED AT the moving silhouette, sweeping across the light in the door, she watched as the figure paused then moved on. Speaking in a language she didn't quite understand. Russian? Something Eastern.

Slowly, she tiptoed along, following Forester towards the open door. The two of them peered into the back of the shop.

Artemis' brow furrowed. Her cheek scraped against the wooden frame, and she felt an icy clot forming in her stomach. Now wasn't the time for breathing exercises or panic attacks. She tried desperately to think of something peaceful. Something tranquil.

What were those damn coping mechanisms her last shrink had given her?

Sixth counselor she'd been through in the last decade. None of them helped much. None of them *knew* her.

She found herself missing that strange sense of warmth she'd felt around Jamie Kramer.

But now, even thoughts of her first crush faded as she stared towards the four men sitting around a long, wooden table. They weren't playing poker or watching horse races or jamming dollar bills into strippers' thongs while glitter scattered like dandruff.

Rather, the four men—each scarier than the next—wearing dark clothing with low hanging collars, were playing a strange game that involved a long, rectangular surface scattered with particles of sand. One of the men had tucked his tongue inside his cheek, was gripping a small, round, metal circle with a plastic handle. He slid the metal circle back and forth on one end of the table and then—aiming—*released*.

The thing slid smoothly across the sand, past three red lines of tape and bumped another similar circle off the table.

A sudden eruption of groaning from the two men on the other side of the table. Artemis wasn't sure what this was. It looked like a miniature game of curling. Perhaps shuffleboard?

She didn't know, nor did she care.

All of the men wore golden necklaces. Two of them had crucifixes. Each of them smelled of strong aftershave, the scent mingling and lingering in the air with the cigarette smoke billowing from the fingers of two of the men.

This back room was far less ornate than the front of the store. A giant, floor-to-ceiling safe with a spinlock sat in the back corner. Besides this, and the shuffleboard, the only other furniture was a small desk with a few chairs crowded around it. Judging by scattered beer bottles beneath these chairs, the men had recently conducted some sort of meeting.

Another small disk was sent spinning across the sandy, wooden surface. This time it fell off the edge.

Another burst of groans from one side of the table, accompanied by cheering on the other.

Artemis just stared in horror. She tried tugging at Forester.

There were too many. Four men against the two of them. And she certainly didn't count. If anything, if it came to a shootout, she'd serve as little more than a moving—and screaming—target.

Forester, though, didn't seem capable of basic math.

He gave her a look, a quick shrug. And then he slipped through the doorway.

"No, don't—"

She tried to protest in a fierce whisper and snatch at his sleeve. But too late. The ataraxic agent was already talking.

"Good evening, gentlemen!" He called out, smiling as he did. He kept his gun holstered.

The four men around the table slowly turned, frowning at him. One of the men, with a golden crucifix around his neck, took a puff on a cigarette and blew the smoke in his direction. Two of the men reached swiftly for their weapons beneath their dark, jacket coats.

"No, no," Forester said quickly. He wasn't raising his gun, though. Instead, his badge was lifted. "We've got you surrounded. I think you knew this day would come. My partner, see her out there, she's a crack shot. Quickest draw I've ever seen. If you reach, she'll dome you both."

Artemis just stared. Never had she heard such whoppers slip so seamlessly from someone's tongue. Forester spoke with conviction, as if he truly believed the lies.

The men who'd been reaching into their jackets hesitated, both glancing towards the smoker with the crucifix. This fellow had white hair at the roots but shoe-varnish black towards the tips, as if he'd dyed it but then given up on maintaining the ruse. His shirt collar revealed more than his fair share of curly chest hair poking up past his gold chain.

"FBI?" this man said, his voice heavily accented. Definitely Eastern European. "What does FBI want with small jeweler shop?" His w's sounded more like v's.

"Upcoming engagement," Forester quipped. "My crackshot? She's also my baby momma. Wants a real big ring."

The two men with their hands in their jackets were glaring now. The one who hadn't spoken or reacted was shifting uncomfortably back at the exchange. He wore glasses and had a purple bow-tie instead of chest hair.

"You," Forester said slowly, pointing a finger at this new figure. "You're the front man?"

"Wh-what?" this fellow said with twice as much stutter but half as much accent.

"Yeah, you are," Forester nodded. "I have a couple questions for you."

"What questions?" snapped the man with the cigarette and chain who Artemis had decided was clearly the head honcho.

Forester shook his head. "Nothing to do with whatever is in that big ol' safe, don't worry. I'm not working organized crime right now."

At this last part, everyone in the room tensed. Artemis could feel the slow, rising sense of anticipation.

"Oh, damn," said Forester. "Did I touch a nerve? I said I'm *not* working organized cri—see, there you guys go again. All shifty-eyed and licky-lipped. It's enough to make a fella uneasy. Let's all simmer down, huh? You know what might help? Let's put those weapons of yours where I can see them. You two—mhmm, grabby hands. Guns on the pool table."

"It's shuffleboard," said the man with the bow-tie and squeaky voice.

"Smart guy, huh? Now, come on—weapons out."

At another nod from the head honcho, the two gun-thugs slowly lifted weapons and placed them on the sandy, wooden surface. Meanwhile, Artemis resisted the urge to turn and run away. She felt nearly *certain* that Agent Grant had *not* permitted any of this. Forester seemed like a seat-of-his-pants type of guy. In a way, it reminded her of Tommy leaping out of that small fishing vessel with treasures still in his pocket.

Now, though, the situation was far less amusing. And if things went wrong it would cost more than a splash of chill water and a few toppled chess pieces in the bottom of a boat.

Forester kept his badge raised, his gun still holstered. She had to hand it to the agent, though. He'd made the call that leading with the FBI logo would get what he wanted faster than his weapon. Perhaps he wasn't as foolish as he initially projected.

Now, though, he was waving his fingers. "Get back, please. Yup, you too, big guy. We're just here for glasses. Yeah—you. I need you to come with us."

The man with the glasses and bow-tie kept shooting panicked looks towards the others. But they were still watching Forester menacingly, occasionally shooting glances towards where Artemis lingered in the door.

And then, suddenly, she felt something warm against the back of her neck. She frowned, began to turn, and then fingers grabbed her throat. A voice spat over her shoulder. "There is no one else. They are alone!"

Panic flared. She tried to shout, but the fingers on her throat held tight. The pain shot up her neck. She tried to swallow, to breath, but realized she was choking. She scrambled desperately with fingers against the tight grip on her throat.

The men by the table surged for their guns.

Forester, though, moved first.

He reached the guns, grabbed them both and *flung* them at the man holding Artemis. One of the weapons hit her elbow. The other, though, judging by the *thunk* and the curse struck center mass over her shoulder. Forester then, like a dancer, redirected.

One motion forward. Grabbed the guns. Flung them.

Next motion back, surging towards Artemis. His long arm shot over her shoulder. The scar along his palm was pale white, and as he extended his hand, she realized the scar crawled all the way up his wrist and forearm and disappeared under the sleeve.

Forester was no longer smiling.

He snatched the man holding Artemis by the throat and *lifted* him bodily, dragging him *over* Artemis.

She just stared, stunned.

Then came the third motion of the violent dance. One second forward, the next back. Then another thrown object.

Except instead of the two guns, this time Forester flung the smaller, heavy-browed individual straight into the head honcho. The two men hit the ground with twin shouts. By now, the two other thugs were charging forward. Fists flew, swiping towards Forester.

But the old fighter stood his ground. He took one blow on the chin, but drove his fist into the belly of the man who'd hit him.

It wasn't a back and forth fight.

Instead, when Forester *hit* the man—straight to the kidney by the look of things—he went pale and collapsed.

The second thug tried to wrap his arm around the agent's neck. But the tall fighter twisted the fingers then twisted the man and sent him stumbling back into the shuffleboard.

"Nobody move!" Forester bellowed, his voice booming. "Except you," he added. He reached out, snagging the man in glasses by the bow-tie, and then *yanked* him back through the door. At the same time, he ushered Artemis away.

"Go, go, go," he said hurriedly. "If I say duck, make sure to—duck!"

He shoved her, hard, sending her sprawling back through the door. Gunfire had erupted behind them. Bullets smashed into glass. Artemis tumbled through the door of the jewelry store, hitting the ground and grazing her palms painfully. At the same time, Forester followed, still dragging the man with the bow-tie.

More gunfire erupted, but Forester had flung the glass door shut.

Two bullets struck where his head had been.

Except the bulletproof glass held firm. White, spiderweb marks of impact spread where the bullets hit.

Artemis was already scrambling back towards the car.

"Get it going!" Forester yelled. "Keys in the ignition!"

She cursed, scrambling into the front seat, turning the key desperately. The car roared to life. She tried to avoid driving as much as possible. It wasn't so much that driving scared *her*. But more like the *other* people who drove that she found terrifying.

As she put the car in gear and slammed the gas, nothing happened.

"You're in neutral!" Forester yelled.

More gunfire. The men were shoving through the glass door now. Artemis, panicked, fingers shaking horribly, managed to put the car in drive. She floored the gas again.

This time, it nearly took them *through* the front of the jewelry store. Instead, she slammed into one of the men who'd been aiming his gun at her. He went flying over the hood, his weapon clattering.

"Nice shot! Reverse now!"

This time, he did it for her. Artemis yelled as she slammed the gas, reversing out of their spot. The rear bumper hit a light post, spitting sparks where it skimmed, but she kept going, speeding hastily away. Only once she was sure the gunfire had stopped did she, with still shaking hands, turn the car in a fast U, hopping the curb with painful *thumps,* and floor the gas, heading rapidly back down the street.

"Hey, Checkers."

"Not now!" she snapped.

"Yeah, but—"

"You are insane. You should be *fired* immediately!"

"Mhmm. I agree, but—"

"I can't fathom how the agency could *possibly—*"

"Checkers, you're on the wrong side of the—yup, there we go."

The vehicle squealed as Artemis narrowly avoided another car heading towards her. She swerved back across the dividing, white line, shaking as the car behind them blared its horn.

She shook her head as she hastened away, muttering darkly beneath her breath. Only then, did she glance in the backseat where Forester was sitting. He still had a firm grip on bow-tie's accessory, holding the mobster in place.

"Good job, by the way," the agent said, nodding. But his voice was somewhat shaky.

"You nearly got me killed," she retorted.

"I... I..." He bit his lip. "I'm sorry."

She stared in the mirror, certain he was teasing again. But he sounded sincere.

"You are?" she asked, surprised.

"Yes. Very sorry. Sometimes things get away from me. I just... I forget that..."

She paused, then glared. "You want something."

"What?"

"Yes, you're being contrite because you want something."

"I—I never—well, now that you mention it. Maybe don't bring this up with Grant?" He winced, forcing a quick smile.

She stared into the rearview mirror until she nearly ran a stop sign. The car jolted to a halt and then slowly rolled through. "You're unbelievable," she said.

"It's just... I'm on a bit of a short leash right now. Some small incident on my last assignment. This was supposed to be a run-of-the-mill interview. So... if you wouldn't mind..."

"I'm telling. Oh, I'm telling them *everything*. You're not safe to work with. You're an absolute liability."

Artemis' hands were shaking nearly as badly as her voice. She knew it was mostly fear talking. Forester *had* handled himself back there. She'd never seen a man fight a room before and win. She'd seen Tommy fight people before, but those altercations usually had ended with her brother eating tarmac.

For Forester to take on four men, though... It reminded her of when she'd first played a blindfolded game. Against five other boards. Five against one, and she'd still scored 5-0.

She knew what it was to feel competent in her own abilities.

But *this* was different. Lives were on the line, and Forester treated it all like some big joke.

"I'm telling Grant," she snapped. "I hope they fire you."

Forester sighed, wincing in the backseat but, this time, holding any further comments.

The man with the bow-tie was slowly propped into a sitting position. She listened to the faint *click-click-CLICK* of the handcuffs as Forester secured man in place. And then, with increasing speed, Artemis sped away from the night-time city, hastening back to more familiar pastures.

Too much concrete. Too much glass. Too many lights and roads...

Too many... people.

She'd always hated the city.

And this was just another reminder of *why*.

And amidst it all, she couldn't forget a very *simple* thing. The killer was still out there. Forester had risked her life. Had put her in danger. But the killer was still out there, and if she wanted to do something about it, she'd have to be present when they spoke to the mobster in the back seat.

12

THEY WERE ONCE AGAIN back in the cold interrogation room, and Artemis desperately wished she could have borrowed a sweater. She crossed her arms and pressed her teeth tightly together.

It was nearly midnight. The precinct was practically empty, which suited Artemis just fine. She didn't want any run-ins with the locals, anyway. Bad blood ran deep in a small town, and she could still remember how they had treated her family more than a decade ago.

"Stop wasting our time," Forester was saying, his hands tapping against the metal table, "Just tell us. Who else knew about the gold? Because if *no* one else did, bud, you're looking at some pretty serious charges over there."

The man across the table shifted uncomfortably. He swallowed, his bow-tie rising and falling. "What gold?" he said in perhaps the least convincing tone he could have managed.

Forester frowned at the man, letting out a faint sigh. They'd already been at it for nearly half an hour.

Each time Forester asked a question, the mobster would respond in feigned surprise. Now, Artemis' eyes were growing heavy. Forester's temper was showing. And the mobster sat, sweat prickling his forehead, Adam's apple bouncing with each heavy swallow.

There was fear in the man's eyes, but the fear had nothing to do with the police station, nor the FBI agent across the table.

Artemis didn't doubt that men like this had a strict code when it came to snitching.

Forester shook his head. "We've got you on a murder rap, buddy. If no one else knew about that gold, then you're the prime candidate. Someone showed up at Mrs. Kramer's house looking for that lil' box of treasure. Someone who knew it was there." He shook his head, tapping a finger against his chin. "And according to her kid, no one knew about the gold except you. And..." his eyes darted towards Artemis. "Your accomplices."

The mobster just shrugged. "No speak English," he said.

"Great," Forester said, throwing his hands up. "That's how you want to be? Two can play at that game. How about a few hours listening to some of my favorite death metal over the speakers in here? Think that will help the sudden onset language amnesia?"

"No," Artemis said quietly.

The two men glanced over at her. She hadn't spoken until now, preferring to simply watch the exchange, to listen. To learn.

And what she'd learned was simple.

The man across the table was very thirsty. Was very scared. And *really* disliked Forester.

On this last part, she felt some level of empathy.

But also, the man in the bow-tie wasn't going to talk. He'd been prepared for this. She could see that much. Even how he hunched in his chair, defensively, how he kept his cuffed hands resting lightly against the metal and adjusted, seamlessly, to accommodate the metal chain. The way he kept glancing towards the camera above the door.

He knew how to conduct himself in a police interrogation.

And so the only way to get someone like that to talk was to change the game being played. He'd prepared for this particular scenario.

And so she said, simply, "Let him go."

Forester blinked. "Excuse me?"

"Just let him go. Don't arrest him again. Don't go back to that store. Let him go and don't do a single thing."

Forester went quiet now, realizing she was making a play of her own.

Artemis wasn't experienced in an interrogation room. But she knew what it was to face a man across a table. Knew what it was to shift openings halfway through. She could see the way his fingers tensed. Could see the quick swallow, the hesitant pause as he held his breath and then quickly released it.

Fear again.

She nodded and looked across the table. He'd prepared for tricks, for tactics. For the police to come with all their usual fare.

But Artemis wasn't police. She didn't know interrogation techniques.

But she knew people.

Sometimes, lying got what was needed.

But other times... Telling the truth was just as powerful. Depending, of course, on what the truth entailed.

"Your boss is going to wonder why we let you go," she said simply. "We're not going to come back. And so for the first few days they'll ask you *why* you were released. You might tell them. You might even mention what I'm saying now. But then? We'll freeze one of your boss's accounts." She decided the narrative use of "we" was stronger than saying, "they."

"Maybe we'll have him pulled over a couple of times. Nothing major. Just enough to get him asking why the FBI keeps harassing him. They're going to wonder what it was you told us. Why, if we keep going after him, did we let one of his men go?"

The man swallowed again, staring at her. She knew when she had a captive audience.

She'd seen captive audiences before. The way they leaned slightly forward in their seats. Even if reclining, it would be in the tilt of their necks, their chins. The angles of their eyes. The direction they stared—how long they held eye contact.

Yes... She knew a captive audience.

"You're not very high up on the totem pole, are you?" she said simply. "You didn't even have a weapon back in that shop. Also, you're the only one who got away without a beating. They're going to wonder about that as well."

"Wait, wait," the man said quickly. "I do not help you. This is lie."

"Yes," Artemis said faintly. "It is. And, honestly, I don't really know what I'm doing here. I wish I was home in bed, sleeping. He scares me as much as he scares you," she added, nodding towards Forester.

"Stupid American no scare me," snapped the man.

Artemis shrugged. "Fine. Then how about we let you go. And... maybe five thousand? Do you think that's how much?" she said, glancing at Forester.

To her surprise, he started nodding, his lips pressed together in thought. "Mhmm. I can make the transfer tomorrow."

"What transfer?" snapped the mobster.

"The money we're putting in your account," Forester replied. "For helping us. Thank you, by the way. From the bottom of my heart." He was smiling now, nodding.

"I—I didn't..." And then his eyes widened in horror as the full weight of their words finally seemed to register.

Artemis wanted to attribute this to a late night and a language barrier. But she was beginning to get the impression that a slow mind was more to blame.

"You will get me killed!" he said, desperate. "They will," he swallowed, "cut me up."

"Possibly," Artemis replied softly. She hated the cold, cool way in which she spoke. For a moment, she wondered if this was how Agent Grant felt when playing with other peoples' lives. But also, she knew what was at stake. This man had sold gold to Mrs. Kramer. Donna had been killed and buried on top of the gold by someone who had known the gold existed but hadn't known where it was. The only two people who knew *where* the gold had been were Mr. and Mrs. Kramer. Which meant the list of suspects was as long as the number of people who knew about the gold.

Tommy, she was certain, would never have done anything like that. He'd always been very fond of Donna as well. Jamie was still his friend judging by the connection he'd made between this mobster and the Kramer family.

"Let me guess," Artemis said slowly. "A discount on the gold? Was it stolen, hmm?"

"No," he snapped. "We are honest businessmen."

"Sure, yes," Artemis said, sighing. "So how about you continue your honest business. And in exchange you help us find someone who's killing people in Pinelake?"

He frowned. "We have not killed anyone in Pinelake."

"It bothers me," Forester muttered, "That you didn't end that sentence at 'anyone.'"

The mobster just sneered.

"What's your name?" Artemis said quietly. "You didn't have ID. What should I call you?"

He paused, snorted. "Vlad," he said.

Forester rolled his eyes.

"Alright, Vlad," Artemis said. "Here's the deal—you tell us who knew about the gold beside you. That's it."

"I sell more than one gold," Vlad snapped. "I not know who you mean."

"The Kramers," Forester interjected. "Donna and Erik Kramer."

No recognition. Artemis said, "The family Tommy Blythe recommended to you."

A flicker of something in his eyes. He swallowed, glancing across the table.

"Maybe we should make it ten thousand," said Forester brightly. "That should raise some eyebrows over at evil-R'-us."

"No, no, wait," snapped the man. "Don't... don't do this." He huffed faintly, muttering to himself in a language Artemis didn't understand. Once upon a time, she'd wanted to start learning languages, but she simply hadn't had the time with all her study.

"You know what they do?" the mobster said quietly. "If I say things?"

"Nothing pleasant, I'd imagine," Forester replied.

"They cut your neck and put your toes down it," he said simply. "Hmm?" He swallowed again. She noticed the lump of his Adam's apple seemed more pronounced than it had before. She winced at the visual image.

He sighed. "Tommy... He have friend who want gold. I sell gold. That all."

"So you are the only one who knew?" Artemis insisted.

"Besides Tommy," Forester added.

"It isn't Tommy," she snapped. "He wouldn't do that. Ever."

Forester just shrugged. He glanced back at Vlad. If anything, the FBI agent almost seemed earnest as he said, "You're sure no one else?"

"I..." And suddenly the man frowned. His hands lowered slowly to the table, flat now. He hesitated, swallowing once. "Man come in two days later."

"A man came to your store?"

"Yes. Tommy give name. Woman and man come in and buy gold," he said.

"Mr. and Mrs. Kramer?"

He nodded.

"And so *another* man came two days later?"

"Yes. Another man come two days later."

"And what did this man want?" Forester asked, leaning forward eagerly.

But the mobster was looking at Artemis now, clearly not wanting to address Forester. "He want," the mobster said, "to know about gold. Where gold. What I sell. He ask about ring."

"Ring?" Artemis asked suddenly. "Like Mrs. Forester's wedding ring?"

The mobster shrugged.

Artemis shot the agent a quick glance. Forester said, "What did this second man look like?"

"Hood, big glass... how you say?"

"Sunglasses?" Forester guessed.

The mobster nodded.

"You just let a man in a hood and sunglasses walk into your jewelry store?" Artemis said, doubtful.

He eyed her for a moment. "Yes... because... *jewelry* store, hmm?"

She hesitated then leaned back in her chair. "Oh. Right. You sell other things, don't you?"

He didn't answer this.

"So you're used to clients showing up hiding their identities," Forester asked. "It's too much to think you might have camera footage, isn't it?"

Now he actually snorted in derision. "No camera."

"How tall was this man? What did he look like from what you could see?" Forester pressed.

"No tall. No short. Thin." He shook his head. "I no know."

"Think! You have to do better than that."

"I *no* know! I no tell him. I tell him scram. I… help him leave."

"You put your hands on him? Did you hit him?" Artemis said quickly.

The mobster nodded quickly. He mimed punching with one hand and pointed towards his own ribs.

"So you punched him in the ribs?" Artemis winced, glancing towards Forester. "Maybe it left a bruise."

"Yes, bruise," said Vlad, sounding quite pleased with himself.

Forester sighed, rubbing a hand across his face, shielding his dark eyes. He leaned back and then crossed his arms behind his head. "It's not like we can just stroll through town asking men to show us their abs," he said with a grunt. "Shit. Come on, Vlad. Give me something. What was he wearing? Shoes? Clothing?"

But Vlad kept shaking his head.

Artemis hesitated, then said suddenly. "Did he have a ring? A necklace? Any jewelry? Come on—you must have noticed something like that. It would be the first thing you looked for."

"First thing look for is gun," snapped Vlad. But then he hesitated, raised his hand and fluttered his fingers. He added a faint mutter.

"What was that?" Artemis said, leaning forward again.

Another grunt, and flutter of fingers.

"Speak clearer," Forester snapped.

"I say he have ring," Vlad retorted. "Big ring. Big number on side. Fake diamond, not real diamond. Fake jeweler glass."

"So he had a big ring on," Forester said. "Any idea where someone might have purchased something like—"

"Football ring," Artemis murmured softly, her voice shaking.

Forester frowned, looking at her. "What?"

"I, er... I think at least," she said, quickly covering. "I mean, maybe. It sounds like a football ring at least." In fact, it sounded *exactly* like a junior varsity championship ring from Pinelake middle school...

Forester frowned. He spoke slowly, but even as he asked, she knew he already had guessed the answer. "Does your brother have one of those rings?"

It was late. She was tired. Her mind exhausted, mentally worn. All she wanted to do now was crawl in bed. Maybe spend a bit of time going over her last game with Stefan. She wanted to call her favorite analysts, the Washingtons. Wanted to lock herself in a room and forget all this nasty business of murder and mobsters.

She swallowed faintly.

And then she lied for her brother. "N-no," she said simply. "No. Tommy doesn't have anything like that. I... I can ask around though. I might find someone who does."

Forester was staring her dead in the eyes. He didn't blink and didn't look away. The tall, handsome man, with the scar along his arm, looked frightening sitting there. She wanted to look away, but knew—in that moment—she couldn't quail.

Because, of course, Tommy had a ring like that. He'd been on the team that had won it, hadn't he? The year before he'd ran away. He'd already been running errands for criminals at that point—making a spare buck.

But her brother *hadn't* done this. She refused to believe it.

She certainly wasn't about to sic Agent Forester on Tommy. She couldn't imagine that horrible interaction. She'd never met two men more stubborn, more self-assured, more willing to live on the fringe and risk becoming some cautionary tale on the nightly news.

Putting them both in the same room would end with one of them dead. She felt certain of it.

No... no, she couldn't tell Forester.

So she kept her expression impassive. The same way she so often did when an opponent had her cornered. Never show weakness.

Weakness gave confidence. Confidence bred courage.

No... She kept emotionless, still. Just shrugged. "I can ask around," she said simply. She forced a quick smile. "It's getting late. Maybe...

maybe we should retire for the night? You can... handle him, yeah?" she winced, waving a hand towards the mobster.

She was a press-ganged consultant. Forced into the position she now found herself in on behalf of her twin brother. But by the looks and sounds of things, Tommy was going out of his way to make it nearly impossible for her to protect him.

More than ever, now, she wished she could have just sent him a damn postcard.

She pushed out of her seat, refusing to meet Forester's searching gaze. When he wasn't joking, there was an off-putting, clever glint in his eyes. She felt a horrible, dreadful certainty that Forester had seen right through the lie.

But she didn't look back. She couldn't show weakness.

She just pushed out of the interrogation room, faking a yawn to sell her indifference, and then allowing the door to swing slowly shut behind her.

Only once the door *clicked* did she stab her hand into her pocket with shaking, trembling fingers. She no longer had Tommy's number. But Jamie would.

She sent a quick text, her fingers flying over the keys.

Need Tommy's number. Urgent. Asap. Please!

Quickly, she hastened down the hall, moving away from the interrogation room with rapid footfalls. As she did, feeling weak-kneed, her phone suddenly vibrated.

She frowned, staring down. Despite the late hour, Jamie had gotten back to her.

She winced as she read the message though.

Number on my work phone. Can I get it to you tomorrow morning? First thing.

She stared, reading and re-reading. Her heart pounded horribly. She wanted to fling her phone across the precinct. But she could feel where a desk sergeant was watching her. Were those eyes that recognized her. She glanced over.

The sergeant was scowling.

She supposed that answered her question.

She looked away again, licking her dry lips nervously. She supposed it wouldn't be the *worst* thing to wait until morning. It was midnight. Even someone like Forester would have to sleep, wouldn't he? Besides, they wouldn't be able to track Tommy down that easily, either. When he'd first ran away, it had taken police nearly six months to find him.

Tommy had a way of squirreling when he wanted.

She let out a faint, fluttering sigh as she stepped through sliding glass doors onto the stairs that led to the parking lot.

She would have to call a taxi or set up a ride on an app.

Tommy could wait... He'd have to wait.

She texted back. *Fine. Thanks. First thing? Please...*

She added a little smiley fa—

Shit. A heart.

Dammit. She quickly tried to tap the icon… But no—it was already sent.

She bit her lip, feeling a flare of anxiety.

Her phone vibrated again.

Jamie texted back.

Really good to see you, by the way. Missed you. Lunch tomorrow?

She stared at the message, standing outside the precinct, facing the main avenue that cut through the heart of Pinelake. Across she spotted the old hardware store. Behind it was the favorite frozen yogurt place that had been in town fifty years now. She spotted a boat rental office at the end of the street and glimpsed a faint shimmer through the trees of the lake beyond. Small homes, quaint, two story patterned the woods in tasteful arrangements.

Pinelake…

Once home.

Now a place that only brought back bad memories.

Then again… not *all* the memories were bad. She stared at the phone. Paused only a second. Then replied.

Yes!

She hesitated, deleted the punctuation and instead went with:

Yes. Great. See you then—just let me know where. Also, please remember Tommy's number."

She sent and lowered the phone, inhaling shakily. Memories came b ack... memories of when things had been better. When life had been... simpler. She'd had a crush on Jamie Kramer long before she'd moved in with them. Long before her sister had died.

One of her psychologists had said she'd been emotionally trapped. The trauma of her sister's death, her father's arrest serving as a sort of prison for her emotions, holding them hostage in memory alone.

She'd never gone back to that particular shrink...

Trapped emotions? What the hell was she supposed to do with that?

And now she'd returned.

Was this what her father had wanted? To lure her back?

She wouldn't have put it past him.

He never asked for the thing he actually wanted. He just used words like levers. And people like pulleys.

She hated the thought of being a puppet on one of his strings.

Hated that somehow, even locked behind bars, he'd managed to rope her back into Pinelake.

And now this business with Tommy...

She felt trapped, like the walls were closing in, and there was nowhere left to run. She needed some sleep. Needed to... to think. To analyze the game. To just spend some time away from precincts, police and everything in between.

She raised her phone again, glancing at the thumbs up message from Jamie—her heart skipped a beat, just like it always had when she'd been younger. But no... no, her emotions weren't trapped. She was. In this terrible town. She sighed then cycled to the internet browser to call a late night taxi.

13

His favorite part, he felt, was the moment of resignation. When they finally realized they were about to die, and there was nothing they could do about it.

He smiled to himself as he slipped through the forest, strolling between the trees and across the ground cover. He inhaled the fresh air under the watch of night, moving in the direction of his new plaything.

He'd spent a while studying her. He knew her habits, her routines. Knew how many showers she took, how many meals she ate. Knew what her favorite color of underwear was. Knew how often she watched the news, and how often she cried herself to sleep.

He liked knowing things. Liked to come prepared.

And this time, he'd done just that.

The first one, drowned. The next one, burned. The most recent one, buried alive.

It was their fear he wanted most. And so this time, he had a new trick up his sleeve. More specifically, clutched under one arm.

A small, brown box, with holes poked in the top. He could feel it moving, the thick, corpulent body shifting about inside the small box. He hadn't thought something so large could fit in such a small package.

Wonders never ceased.

In fact, he had caught this delightful little thing himself. He wondered how Ms. Ortega would react.

The sheer thought of her terror gave him a giddy little shiver. He liked the way they trembled, begged. Some people thought the young and the voluptuous were the pinnacle of beauty. But in his mind, maturity was just as gorgeous as smooth skin and a perky disposition.

His first victim had been twenty-three. The next one thirty-five. The last one, Donna Kramer, had been fifty. And now came Ms. Ortega. She was in her forties. Each of them had qualities he had enjoyed. Each of them displayed panic in their own unique way.

The creature in the small box was now shifting violently, protesting the motion. He stroked the box, murmuring, "Almost there. Almost there."

He emerged from the forest, stepping out of the trees and peering up towards the large mansion.

Such a big home for one woman.

Of course, it had been home to more than one person only a month ago. Things had turned sour with Ortega's lover.

But a house that big provided more than one entry point. He had already studied the security system. Already picked out which window. He knew the one she left open for a faint summer breeze.

He moved across the lawn, the leaves and sticks fading to soft grass, as if even the yard was helping him move silently.

The box continued to shake, shift. He kept murmuring soothingly, stroking it. He stared at the small open window on the first floor.

Perfect.

Just like he had planned.

This time, it wouldn't be buried. But, of course, like with everyone else, he had to make sure she had what he thought she did. Once he found it, that's where he would put the body, and that was when his little friend would be released from its confines.

He didn't even crouch, as he knew no one else would see them. He simply walked, his shadow cast back by a flickering porch light. He moved directly towards the open window, his mouth moist with anticipation.

14

Exhaustion weighed on her, and Artemis was already regretting her decision not to report Forester. She stuck by her initial assessment. That man was a loose cannon.

Then again she had agreed to work as a consultant. Had agreed to go with him to a known mobster's location. She had refused to accept the weapon he had handed her.

But she wasn't trained. She had been strong-armed into this by Grant. Her brother had been threatened. Still, she wasn't sure she would have been able to keep herself from rocking the boat if not for Jamie.

She felt a flicker of excitement, forcing back a smile. He wanted to grab lunch. It was a scenario she had rehearsed a million times. Lunch with Jamie Kramer.

The only person in all of Pinelake who didn't hate her guts.

She pushed through the door of the small hotel. When she had arrived, the items from the place she'd been staying at in Seattle had been on her bed. She didn't like the idea of someone snooping in her belongings, not even to bring them to her.

But she could only fight one battle at a time.

Most of all, she had missed her computer.

Once she had double checked the locks on her hotel room door and she clicked on the small lamp at the end table, she settled at the foot of her bed, using the footboard as a backrest. She unzipped her laptop, pulled out the device, and booted it up.

An angled, laminated note next to the bed displayed the Wi-Fi password.

She logged into her computer, quickly opening the tabs she usually visited after a game.

Her eyes scanned over blogs and videos critiquing the match. Praise flooded in. She smiled as one of the leading analysts said in a clip, "...one of Blythe's more impressive wins."

Praise in the chess world could be somewhat stilted, but she took it where she could get it.

A few members from her streaming community were raving about the victory. She tried not to spend too much time scrolling through the comments, but she couldn't resist. For years, she had trained for these moments. She thought back to Helen and her sister's big dreams. Helen had always been smarter, though sometimes, Artemis had wondered if this had simply been a factor of age.

She would never know. Helen had disappeared two years before the news broke about their father. Before Artemis had noticed the discrepancy on the news. She hadn't known what the clue she'd provided would lead to. And when it showed up at her door, accompanied by flashing red and blue lights and blaring sirens, it had shattered her world.

But not nearly as horribly as the night when Helen vanished.

Artemis had never gotten him to admit it. In fact, when she had asked him, while he was being led away in cuffs, he had denied having anything to do with it.

But she knew her father had killed her sister. He had targeted women just like Helen. Smart, clever, competent and successful. He'd killed seven that they knew of. But Artemis knew there were more. Helen had only been fifteen at the time of her disappearance.

When Helen had first vanished, Artemis had held onto hope. At the time, she hadn't known what her father was.

He had played them all for fools. He had taught them to study, to watch, to listen and observe. But the one person she hadn't applied the lessons to had been the one who had most severely betrayed them.

She frowned as these memories flickered past, her eyes staring sightless at the computer screen.

Her father seemed normal to her. Charming, theatric, intelligent. She hadn't realized what sort of chameleon he really was until too late.

There were some in the FBI who suggested her father had been actively murdering for more than twenty years. Some suggested the body count was closer to fifty.

She had never looked too closely. Instead, she had retreated into chess. The one game that made sense. The one thing she could control.

Besides, Helen was the one who had dreamed of becoming a world champion. The first woman to ever do it. That had been Helen's goal, and so Artemis had taken another step, winning the Seattle Open, on her path to making a sister proud who she would never see again.

She leaned back, listening to the faint whir of the fan above her bed. Her head pressed into the covers draping over the edge.

The hard floor was strangely comforting to her. From the age of thirteen until sixteen, she had lived in more than one foster home with little more than blankets on a stiff cot. She had learned to deal with discomfort.

Suddenly, a small, green bubble appeared in the bottom of her computer screen.

She frowned, watching the flashing indicator.

Someone was calling. It took her a second, but then she recognized the name of one of her favorite analysts.

She smiled and quickly answered.

Two smiling faces stared out at her. Mr. and Mrs. Washington were both chess aficionados and internationally ranked masters themselves. They were no longer playing in tournaments, and neither had ever broken the top 100, but they were brilliant, and, more importantly, Artemis was very fond of them.

The married couple were the first people who had ever analyzed one of the games she had posted online. They had come back with some strong criticism over some of her opening moves. But they had done it in such a kind, friendly way, she hadn't been able to hold it against them. If anything, they had reminded her of Helen.

Now, the older couple were both smiling into their web camera. Mrs. Washington was adjusting the screen. Mr. Washington, in his deep, bass voice kept saying, "Leave it alone, Cynthia."

"It's not focusing, Henry," she replied firmly.

Artemis cleared her throat. "Hey, guys!"

The webcam went still. The two analysts leaned back on their pink couch. Behind them, a large tapestry displayed small pictures that had been drawn by their grandchildren.

Something about that image had always filled Artemis with a strange sense of emptiness.

But then, she would look at the Washingtons, how they sat so close to each other on the couch, still in their sixties, having been married for nearly forty years, and she couldn't help but smile.

She had never met them in real life. One day, she hoped this could change.

"Artemis, dear!" said Cynthia, beaming, "You did it!"

Artemis smiled, nodding, and brushing a strand of hair behind her ear.

Henry was frowning, his eyes off to the side. "Why the queen sacrifice?" He muttered. "You still had the fork without it."

Cynthia nudged her husband. "Come on, Henry, be nice."

He looked up, and when his eyes found the camera, he smiled, the wrinkles from his frown melting. "Well done, though," he said with a nod. "Tough opponent. Though, did you notice they stiffed you on ranking points?"

Artemis frowned. She typed quickly into the browser. She pulled up the status of her rank and then scowled. "That's five points less. How does that make sense?"

"Sexism," Cynthia said, firmly. "They're trying to keep you down, Artemis. Don't let them. I'll write a letter to the director myself."

Henry, in that slow, deep voice of his said, "Now, now, let's not be hasty. Did you read the article? It looks like the last opponent Wright faced was found cheating. There was a discussion about how that should affect his ranking. Unfortunately, there was a ripple effect."

"If this was Anton there never would have been a ripple effect," said Cynthia, pursing her lips and shaking her head side to side. Her pale hair swished across wrinkled, dark skin.

Artemis winced at the name of the world champion. Anton Radesh was Indian-Italian, both of his parents also renowned in the chess world. He had started playing at the age of six. He had won his first tournament when he'd been nine. To this day, he was still the youngest player to ever achieve Grandmaster.

Artemis was determined to one day beat him. There was no opponent she studied nearly so much as Anton.

But the man was a machine. At 28 now, he'd been world champion five years running. He had nearly broken 3000 rating points, something never before done. He was always the favorite to win. As many analysts often quipped, at any tournament Anton played in, 49 players fought for second place.

And though she had won a regional tournament, she was still far from being considered a serious contender.

"What did you think about the opening?" she said, redirecting the conversation.

"Defensive. I prefer D6 myself," Henry replied.

"Artemis," his wife cut in. "Develop your knights earlier, dear."

Artemis paused. "That makes sense. But I was trying to get his bishop out early. I didn't want him to pin me."

The Washingtons considered this, and Henry began pointing at his screen, which he often did, as if he didn't realize she couldn't see what he was indicating. But Artemis could replay the game in her head, so she watched the board in her mind's eye, letting the analyst talk her through his thoughts.

Cynthia and her husband had vastly different play styles. Henry was more cautious, meticulous. Cynthia liked aggressive openings. Sometimes, she would sacrifice material for advantage.

Artemis didn't really mind if she agreed or disagreed with their tactics. She always went away from these conversations having learned something. But most importantly, she simply liked talking to them. It felt... warm.

Not quite the same warmth as Jamie Kramer but similar in temperature, though, not intensity. It was hard for her to describe.

Sometimes, she would nod and frown, doing her best to look serious. But all she really wanted to do was watch the Washingtons on the couch, forcing back a smile at the way Cynthia would tap at her husband's forearm. Or the way Henry would pat his wife on the knee when he wanted to interrupt and make a point.

Artemis wondered what it was like to have been married for forty years. She was thirty, and besides Jamie Kramer, she hadn't dated anyone.

There, locked in the hotel room, smiling at the computer screen, the faint clot in her chest lessened somehow.

It was no way to live, scared of the world.

But if anyone had a right to their terror, she felt it was her.

Artemis listened as the two analysts continued, nodding along, and playing the game out in her memory once more. Cynthia even spotted a blunder that Stefan had missed. Artemis had spotted the mistake during the game but had felt her opponent wouldn't capitalize. She had already taken him too deep.

She sighed, simply enjoying the familiar voices over the computer speakers.

Safe, protected, she never wanted to leave.

But eventually, like always, Cynthia would get tired, or Henry would want to catch his show. He liked watching blacksmiths make swords on a reality TV show. His wife had called it the bachelorette for nerds.

And so, often, Artemis couldn't enjoy the conversations as they went on. Because she felt herself so often anticipating their end.

But as she settled, shoulders against the footrest of her bed, legs curled up like a butterfly's wings under her, she couldn't help her mind from wandering.

She was back in Pinelake. The Ghostkiller's daughter had returned home. Only to find more deaths amidst the trees and beneath the mist. She let out a faint sigh.

Their interrogation of the mobster hadn't taken them anywhere useful. No footage, no security cameras. She supposed this made sense. But his loose description of the man who had asked about the gold wasn't helpful... Except that damn ring.

Hopefully, Jamie would text her Tommy's number early in the morning.

Artemis had agreed to help Agent Grant. Had given her word to aid in solving the case. And now Jamie wanted to get a meal.

This town had its hooks in her. Was this what her father had intended all along?"

She scowled, and Cynthia, thinking it was something she had said, quickly added, "I don't mean it was a bad move. I just think castling queen-side would have been stronger."

Artemis nodded quickly, masking her expression.

The killer was still out there. Grant seemed to think he would strike again, and despite her calculating demeanor, they were no closer to catching the man.

Artemis had a brief thought that sent shivers up her back. If her father had managed to lure her back, even while in prison, maybe he wasn't as ignorant as she had thought. What if he did know something about the case?

She shook her head, though, and quickly passed it off as if she were rubbing her neck.

No. No, she refused to talk to that man. Besides, she could figure something else out. She had found a lead, hadn't she? They had arrived at a dead end, but she could find another lead. She would have to.

It wasn't Tommy. It *couldn't* be Tommy.

She nodded, slowly, settling in, certain she would talk chess well into the night.

She didn't want to go to bed yet. If she did, it would only make morning come faster... And then she would have to figure out how to prove her brother wasn't involved in this mess.

15

Eight-year-old Artemis shifted uncomfortably next to Helen, watching the people file into the small theater. Her sister, a teenager, watched the crowd with some level of disdain. Helen had always been the smarter of the two Blythe girls, but one wouldn't have known it in how she lauded Artemis.

But this didn't stop her from the occasional posture of "instructor."

"What about him?" Helen said, nodding towards a man with a cane. The old man had wispy facial hair and blinked rapidly behind glasses two sizes too large for his face. He wore a flat cap and walked with a limp, leaning on the cane with a wizened hand.

Artemis studied the man from where she stood in the back of the room, peering through the glass screen of the small sound booth. "He's... I... I don't know," Artemis said slowly.

This answer was never unwelcome.

Helen nodded once. "Alright. It's good to admit when you don't know. Pay closer attention, though. Remember what dad told us last year?"

Artemis hesitated, wrinkling her nose. She shifted in the light, baby blue dress with bows along the front. She hated the dress. Hated the clip-on earrings and the curls in her hair. But her father insisted that when they were working, they made an impression.

Helen had managed to avoid the frills—her dress was sleek, dark and, in Artemis' opinion, *very* beautiful. In fact, everything about Helen was beautiful. Everyone said so.

After a few particularly obnoxious comments from drunk audience members, Helen now carried a small can of pepper spray and a miniature switch-blade Tommy had provided for her. Both were hidden in her dress.

And while Helen had avoided the frills, she hadn't been able to avoid the curls. Her hair was naturally wavy, a mane of cascading bronze. How often had Artemis seen her sister tug at one of her bangs, scowling at some puzzle or problem.

And now, her finger was out, curling around a long loop of hair, and she was frowning in the direction of the old man. "You're missing something, Art," murmured Helen. Only Artemis' sister, and Tommy on rare occasions, was allowed to use this pet name for her. She meant it as a compliment.

"I..." eight-year-old Artemis shifted uncomfortably, frowning. And then her eyes suddenly brightened. "He's faking the limp." She shot a quick look towards her sister.

More folks streamed through the open double doors at the back of the theater, moving towards their seats. The red padded, faux wood seats were soon filled. The stage they faced was currently empty, but the flickering light above the stage, casting strobing patterns of illumination across the audience, was mesmerizing.

Like moths to a flame, her father often said.

"And how do you know he's faking the limp?" asked Helen, leaning forward on the desk and beginning to twist at some of the knobs on the soundboard. The two girls were in charge of audio for the evening. Tommy was supposed to be the usher. But their eight-year-old brother was nowhere to be seen. Artemis' twin often went missing.

The two of them may have shared a birthday, but that was where the similarities ended.

"Where's Tommy?" Artemis asked.

"Probably stealing things from the coat room. Now focus, Art—why do you know he's faking his limp."

Now that she saw it, the trick was obvious enough. Artemis had smoothed at a couple of her bows. A small red light was blinking on the soundboard, suggesting their father was about to step on stage. A low hush of anticipation was beginning to fall over the crowd.

"Because," Artemis said quietly. "The shoes. They're both equally worn. He doesn't prefer either foot."

Helen grinned. "Anything else?"

"Umm... Umm..." Artemis felt a flush of anxiety. She hated unanswered questions. She began biting at her lip, feeling a sudden jolt of pain. What was she missing? What was... "I don't know," she said again, feeling a surge of disappointment.

Helen chuckled. "You're looking too closely. Sometimes the answer is obvious. Don't be too clever for your own good."

And then Artemis grinned. "Oh. Ha. He's limping with his left now. Back there, he was limping with his right leg."

"Exactly." Helen was pushing a dial on the soundboard all the way up now. The strobing light over the stage had suddenly flared bright, casting shadows across the gathered audience. The faint murmurs and whispers faded to thick anticipation.

"Hang on..." Artemis said suddenly. She glanced at her sister sitting next to her in the sound booth. She plucked at one of the ribbons on her dress. "How did you know about the shoes? You're sitting too far to see them."

Helen grinned now. "One of these days," she said, "you're going to outfox me, you know that?"

Artemis paused, and then her eyes widened. "You knew he was faking before he ever entered..."

"He's dad's plant for tonight," said Helen in distaste. "I saw them speaking last night."

"That's cheating!"

"No. It's a sure bet. You can be the best card-player in the world, Art. But if someone stacked the deck, you'll lose every time. Now hush. Here he comes."

A sudden explosion of applause as a dark figure emerged from behind a ruffling, velvet curtain.

The applause turned into a sudden loud retort. Artemis jerked up, her head bouncing off the foot rest. Her laptop screen had gone dim where it rested on her legs. She had fallen asleep studying yesterday's game.

Another loud burst of knocking. She blinked, frowning towards the door.

"Artemis!" a voice barked. It was Forester.

"What?" she called back in a morning croak. She frowned. "How did you find me?"

"There is exactly one hotel in this town," Forester retorted. "It wasn't hard."

"Why are you harassing me?"

His tone, though, was completely devoid of its usual humor. "We have another body. Grant wanted me to take you with. Are you coming or no?"

Artemis felt a shiver at these words. Another body? He had killed again?

She wanted to refuse. But she was in too deep. She had given Jamie her word. She let out a faint sigh. "I'm coming, just give me a second."

She shoved roughly to her feet, placing her laptop gently on the bed that she hadn't slept in.

And then she hastened to get dressed, feeling that same prickle of ice along her spine that she had sensed the night before. When she checked her phone, Jamie still hadn't texted her brother's number.

16

ARTEMIS STARED AT THE body, a faint chill trembling down her spine.

The police moving throughout the crime scene spoke in what felt like hushed voices. It was a large room, in likely the largest home Artemis had ever set foot in. The body of Kateline Ortega reclined in a porcelain hot tub, one arm draped over the side, fingers dangling towards the onyx-tiled floor. A large, resplendent window faced the mountains, providing a framed view of rustling trees and green slopes.

Artemis felt faint, her cheeks prickling as the blood drained from her face.

"Dear God," she murmured beneath her breath. Forester stepped past her, his countenance grim. Supervising Agent Grant could be heard further down the hall, screaming at one of her subordinates. Forester brushed past a man in a white jacket and stared into the tub.

"That thing dead?" he muttered.

The woman nodded. "Suffocated. By the victim."

Forester rubbed a hand over his features. "Christ. It killed her, then she landed on it?"

"Yes."

Artemis could see the tail of the snake from where she stood. She could see the pale, wide-eyed look of terror on the dead woman's features.

The snake was patterned with red and gold spots all along its slick body. The thing was as long as the woman's leg; Artemis had only taken one glance before retreating back towards the door. The snake's slick form draped like a dead tree branch, angled into the tub and then up where its motionless, scaled head rested against the woman's shoulder.

"It's... it's horrible," Artemis whispered, swallowing as she spoke.

Forester glanced at her but gave a quick nod. "Very," he murmured. "Necklace," he said. "Rings. You were right. Killer is leaving their jewelry intentionally on the bodies."

Artemis had spotted the diamond necklace and the colorful rings as well. The necklace wasn't *worn* so much as pooled on the woman's bare chest. The rings had been placed on the fingers but not all the way, only down to the second knuckles. The fingers were too swollen to allow them to slip much further.

Artemis was trying her best not to lose it. But her stomach was now twisting tightly. The familiar lump in her chest was growing. It felt as if a giant had reached down and pinched her lungs. Now, as she breathed, she didn't find the air she so desperately needed.

Her eyes moved away from the corpse. She spotted some soap dispensers along the tub. A bath bomb. And also a pile of books. Literary books, by the looks of them. Though she didn't have a *very* long look. She did glimpse titles. *Anna Karenina. The Great Gatsby* and also *The Invisible Man.*

She ripped her gaze away, trying to focus.

Light-headed, she rocked on her heels. "I... I think the killer..." she swallowed, trying to force herself to soldier on. "I think the killer put the rings on her... after..." But she was breathing too shallowly now to continue. She held up a finger and then turned, stumbling back through the bathroom door.

She fled the horrible scene of the dead woman, the jewelry and the snake. Her footsteps echoed in her ears as she stumbled into the hall, slamming her hands against a wooden banister overlooking a chandelier dangling towards the first floor. Agent Grant was stalking up the stairs now, speaking hurriedly to Wade who strolled alongside.

Artemis pushed off the lacquered rail, and retreated further, footsteps muted by the thick carpet. She shoved into a side room, but realized she'd found a broom closet. By the looks of things, none of the brooms had ever been used. No supplies on the shelves either. A house like this—Artemis didn't doubt that a cleaning crew had been hired.

She stood in the closet now, the door half-cracked. She didn't mind the dark nearly so much. Driving, crowds, cities, dead bodies... She was adding to an ever-expanding list of things she loathed.

But sometimes close spaces, dark corners were the best place to allow her mind to relax. There wasn't much to scrutinize or analyze in a cupboard.

She focused on her breathing, slow, shallow huffs of air. She tried to slow the rapid gasps. In for five seconds. Out for seven. But even this was difficult when her chest started collapsing.

"Shit, shit, dammit," she muttered beneath her breath. Another round of panic shooting through her.

The attacks were physical things. She could feel them in her chest like clots. It wasn't so simple to just *breathe* easier. It wasn't as simple as *thinking about something else.* She'd received all sorts of advice over the years. Ranging from the use of an inhaler to listening to calming music. She knew many people who swore by their favorite remedies.

But for Artemis, the darkness helped.

She could feel her mouth shaking, her lips dry from the constant stream of panting air. She wished she could cry—she could feel the way her cheeks twisted up, but the tears never came. She hadn't cried since the age of thirteen.

Sometimes she missed it. Sometimes it felt as if the emotions were simply left buried deep, unexhumed, skeletons in a closet...

Perhaps much like *this* closet. And Artemis a different type of skeleton.

She leaned back, head against the metal shelves. Whenever a panic attack started, it was difficult to know how long it might last.

One of the worst parts about the attacks was that she could never quite tell *when* they would trigger. One of her greatest fears playing live games in tournaments was the idea that she might one day have an attack in the middle of a match.

So far, thankfully, it had yet to happen.

"Come on," she muttered to herself, her foot tapping a tattoo into the floorboards. "Come on... Come on..." She swallowed desperately, just willing it to pass.

The waiting was the painful part. There had been a time, when she'd been younger, when she would have as many as seven to eight attacks per day. Now, as she'd grown older, distanced from city life, often stuck to her room—away from people—more than was perhaps advisable, she'd found ways to manage. To cope.

She slowly lowered to the ground, arms clutching at her legs, breathing in quick puffs, but trying her best to focus on the breathing exercises.

Tap. Tap.

She froze, more rapid breathing. She looked up, staring at the gap in the door.

"Ms. Blythe?" said Forester slowly. "Are you alright?"

"Go away," she said quickly. It took her a second to even summon the energy to speak the words. She could tell this attack was going to be a bad one. It wasn't common to end up in an emergency room, but it had happened before. Especially if she wasn't given a chance to calm down.

"Can I help?" Forester said quickly. "Anxiety? Panic—my mother used to have those."

"Just—just, please," she said, her voice shaky. "I... I can't..." She couldn't breath again. She watched where Forester lingered outside the door for a moment. She heard him give a faint sigh.

"Cam!" called Grant's voice. "Where is Ms. Blythe? I thought you said you were bringing her."

Artemis could feel her stomach turning horribly. *No, no, no* she thought, her mind screaming. She didn't want to talk to Grant. Couldn't talk. Her lungs just weren't working. Black spots were now dancing across her vision.

Dammit. A bad one. She didn't want to end up in the hospital. She still needed to meet Jamie for lunch. Needed to talk to her stiff-necked brother about what he'd gotten himself involved in.

But as these thoughts circled her mind, she couldn't shake the horrible image seared in her mind. A snake in the bathtub. Jewelry across pale, cold skin. A woman's face twisted in a horrible, silent scream of terror.

"Cam!" Grant shouted. "Where is she?"

Please... please... She thought, but she just didn't have the air to speak.

"No clue," Forester called back. "Probably went outside for a second. It's not pretty up here. Might as well get it over with—let me show you."

Forester left, his shadow moving as he slipped away from the door. His heavy footfalls creaked against the floorboards as he retreated.

She felt a flash of gratitude for the strange agent. Maybe it wasn't so bad she hadn't turned him in. That didn't mean she thought he was a safe person to partner with. As long as she had a say, she would never go into any dangerous parts of the city with the tall man ever again.

But at least for the moment...

She couldn't help but feel grateful,

She closed her eyes, hunched in the dark closet, arms wrapped around her legs. She started murmuring beneath her breath. "D4. D5. Knight F3. E6. Knight C3..." As she recited the game, one that had ended in a draw, the patterns, the familiar movements, the image in her brain of the sixty four black and white squares on the board helped her mind relax.

She focused on the moves, reciting them out loud, watching a movie play out in her mind. As the images unfolded, she felt the clot in her chest loosen slowly. "...Bishop takes," she murmured. "Castle King-side."

And slowly, her body trembling, she was able to breath again. The black spots faded from her vision, and she was able to inhale deeply, feeling the satisfying swell of her lungs. Her chest rising and falling in slower motions.

For a brief moment, she felt a prickle of peace. She almost wanted to sleep now. It was strange just how *relaxing* it could be to breath again. So many people took the air in their lungs for granted.

She didn't have that luxury. 22,000 breaths per day. 960 breaths per hour. 16 breaths per minute. Each of them a sheer gift. None of them earned.

And so it was an unusual cruelty, she thought, to ever take someone's gift of breath.

So far, though, the killer had taken four women's lives. She felt her scowl returning now. Her hand bunched at her side, and she pushed slowly, on shaky legs, back to her feet. Her hand still closed in a fist reached out and pushed open the door.

She stepped back into the hall, exhaling slowly. She peered towards the open door of the large bathroom with the porcelain hot tub on the onyx tiles.

Voices echoed in the room beyond. What she'd been intending to tell Forester before the sudden panic attack had been about the rings. The killer had likely put them on his victim *after* the murder. A pattern was starting to develop.

She couldn't quite say exactly what at this point. But a pattern was certainly forming. She frowned... She still needed more information.

She approached the door now, refusing to enter the gruesome crime scene again. It wasn't like she needed to. One of the downsides of having a longer-term, eidetic memory: she wouldn't forget the image of the dead woman. No matter how hard she tried or wanted to.

Nothing would scrub it free.

She called into the bathroom. "Ah, excuse me?"

She heard muttering, then footsteps. A second later, Agent Grant and Agent Wade appeared in the door. Forester lurked behind them, occasionally looking over, but pretending like he wasn't. He had a distinctly guilty expression where he watched out of the corner of his eye.

He probably didn't know she'd decided not to rat him out to Grant.

Still, it was nice to see the man squirm for a change. Especially after what he'd put her through back in Seattle.

She didn't look towards Forester but, instead, addressed Grant.

"I think I might have an idea," she said simply. "Did you dredge the lake near the first victim?"

"The drowned woman?" Grant asked, frowning. "There was a diving team."

"Did they find anything?"

"Not that I've been made aware of..." Grant pressed her lips together. Her stenciled, thin eyebrows flickered. "Though, we have been having some difficulty with certain officers in this town."

Before or after you brought me home? Artemis thought to herself. Out loud, though, she said, "I'm going to guess the boat was expensive."

"Ah—I couldn't say—"

"Three Wins S-series," Forester called from where he stood in the room. A flash of light illuminated the tiles behind him, suggesting one of the coroner's assistants was now taking photos. "It's expensive," he said. "Brand new it's about two hundred thousand."

Grant glanced back at Artemis. "Well," she said, "there's your answer."

Artemis sighed, nodding. "He's targeting them for their wealth. The jewelry, the mansions. The fancy boat. He's envious. Or greedy."

"Yes," Grant said slowly. "Forester mentioned the same theory yesterday."

Artemis shifted uncomfortably, shooting a glance towards the ex-fighter. She swallowed, thinking slowly. "It's... he wants them to suffer, though. It makes me think that maybe he has something personal against them. Like maybe they remind him of someone." Her mind flashed back to her father. All of his victims had been so similar to Helen, his oldest daughter. Helen had disappeared first. Artemis still believed she'd been her father's first victim. Though he'd never admitted it—not even when he'd been given life without parole.

"So you believe the killer has something against someone like our victims?"

Artemis wasn't sure what else to say. It wasn't like she was the professional here. Wade looked bored, and was glancing off out a window as if he couldn't care less what she had to say. Forester still looked nervous, as if he were expecting Artemis to rat him out at any moment.

To Grant's credit, though, Artemis wasn't a trained agent... Though she wasn't on the FBI team. Though she'd never solved a case... The older woman still listened intently, as if anything Artemis said was worth hearing.

She'd noticed this about the pale-haired leader. She didn't like Grant. Especially not after the threats concerning her brother. But she had to respect the woman's ability to put ego aside and take input from all channels. It was starting to make sense why Cameron Forester was allowed to work under her. Everything was geared towards results with this woman.

A sociopath? It didn't matter. As long as he solved cases.

A complete stranger with no experience whatsoever, hated by the very town she now found herself in? Again, it didn't register. Grant listened as if Artemis were a professor at Harvard giving a lecture.

Even when Wade occasionally spoke, Grant would listen.

Artemis felt as if what she were saying was somewhat obvious, but she wasn't sure exactly how to contribute without walking through her thought process. So, trying not to stammer, she said. "The first victim was found near an expensive boat. Her personal belongings left folded nearby. The second victim was found in her car, jewelry intentionally stowed in the back seat. Mrs. Kramer was buried above a pot of gold. And Ms. Ortega"—a horrible flash of the image in the room beyond.

Artemis swallowed.

"Ms. Ortega," she tried again, "is in the largest mansion on the block, covered in diamonds and jewelry. The killer doesn't *take* any of the expensive items. He prefers leaving them buried... almost like..." She wrinkled her nose. "Like some viking. Or Pharaoh. Left in a tomb with all their earthly possessions."

"So why Ms. Ortega?" Forester called out. "Why not the Mitchells next door? Why skip a house? Is he just picking wealthy women randomly?"

"Crimes of opportunity?" Wade grunted, still sounding bored but at least participating now.

Grant glanced between all of them, and her eyes settled on Artemis again. "I... I don't know how he's picking them," she said at last with a resigned sigh. "They've all lived in the area for a while. They're all different ages... And..."

She bit her lip, trailing off.

"What is it?" Grant said, studying Artemis.

"I... nothing," she said quickly. "Well... I mean, it's stupid. But..." Artemis frowned. "Those books," she said. "The ones next to the tub."

"What about them?"

Artemis hesitated. "They're... they're kind of... what some would call sophisticated."

"Others might say pretentious," Forester quipped.

"And?" Grant pressed.

"And..." Artemis bit her lip. "There's... Hmm... It might be nothing, but... the evidence list. The items found by Mrs. Burrows' boat where she was drowned. There was a book. *The Invisible Man.*"

Forester was frowning now, scrolling through his phone. But then he snapped his fingers. "She's right," he said. "The first victim had the same book."

Artemis sighed. "And back at the precinct, Jamie Kramer mentioned his mother was involved in a pretentious book club. His words, not mine."

Grant frowned, wrinkling her nose. "You think these women are in a book club together?"

Artemis shrugged. "I mean... if they are, I know where it would be hosted. Small towns don't change. And women from this part of town will gather in the same spot—I saw it on the way here."

"What spot?"

"A country club. Very fancy, super exclusive." Artemis shivered in revulsion. "My own brand of hell."

"A book club in an exclusive lodge?" Grant asked, frowning. "You think somehow the killer is targeting members in this book club?"

"I mean... it's possible," Artemis said, wincing. She pictured the pile of books next to the bathtub. "You know, it's probably nothing."

Forester glanced at Grant. "You want me to babysit the consultant or check for security?"

Grant hesitated, glancing between the two of them. Then, she nodded as if reaching a decision. She turned swiftly, having gleaned what she could and now facing her pitbull of a subordinate. "Wade, make sure we get prints from the jewelry. Look for any cameras through the house—places like this have to have security. And Forester, don't just linger. Be useful. Call the security company—see if anything disturbed the house last night, and please escort *Ms.* Blythe to this lodge. We're doing this one by the book."

"Cool thing," Forester said. "Road trip." He glanced at Artemis. "What's the... shall we say, *average age* of the hot, rich ladies at this lodge?"

Artemis paused, shrugged. "Ninety-five, maybe," she said. "They'll *love* you."

"Forester," Grant called. "One moment—Ms. Blythe, he'll meet you outside. A word please, Cameron."

Forester nodded and turned back towards the pale-haired woman.

Artemis, meanwhile, was slowly moving back towards the stairs. As instructions were issued to the FBI agents, she made good her getaway. Moving slowly at first but then picking up speed as she took the stairs two at a time.

She'd wait for Forester in the parking lot. The *Invisible Man.* She shivered. The reason they called her father the Ghostkiller was because—save that one mistake with the dead woman in his bed—most his crimes had been committed without leaving a trace, in locked homes, strangling his victims slowly to leave as little damage as possible. Just like an invisible man.

A coincidence?

She felt a chill.

Her father was in prison. She knew that much. Besides, it was just a hunch. The book club connection might not be *anything...*

At least, that's what she wanted to tell herself.

The idea of rubbing elbows with these women in their fancy country club was already giving Artemis anxiety.

The police sergeant had been nasty.

But the women at the Elk Lodge could be downright vicious.

17

Artemis hastened beneath the glistening chandelier. The house was so very big. Too big—too much space. She missed her bedroom back home. Her small apartment. She missed the dark. Missed playing her favorite game.

The pieces in this game were far harder to analyze, and she didn't have a clue how to move them.

She pulled her phone from her pocket, picking up the pace, moving hastily out the front door towards a row of SUVs circling the parking lot. Local police moved about. She immediately stared at the ground, refusing to meet their glances.

"Come on," she murmured as the phone connected. "Come on," she said, louder, tapping a finger against her thigh. The ringing continued. Why wasn't he picking up? With Forester upstairs for the moment, she had a chance to get Tommy's number. To clear this business about the ring right up. Still, the coincidence was gnawing at her. Of course, Tommy wasn't a killer—she knew that... Didn't she?

"Come on..." she repeated, willing her phone to connect. Why wasn't Jamie answering?

"Hey!" A voice called towards her from behind one of the SUVs.

She looked determinedly away, pretending she hadn't heard.

"Hey, Ghost-girl, I'm talking to you!"

She let out a faint sigh, glanced over and grimaced, pointing to her phone and shrugging apologetically. She spotted a man that it took a moment to recognize. A big man with no neck. He had no hair and looked something like a boulder crossed with a brick wall. He wasn't as athletic-looking as Forester, nor as muscled as Agent Wade. A lot of this man's size came, no doubt, from six-packs of a less impressive variety.

But also he was scowling right at her. He slowly shut the door to his vehicle. The man's partner—a slim, reedy fellow with small glasses—was also emerging from the vehicle. The moment he noticed the thickset fellow's attention, the small man let out a weary sigh as if resigning himself to whatever came next.

"Hey... Why are you here?" the cop demanded.

She recognized him now. He'd been in the same year as Jamie and Tommy at school... at first. Then he'd been held back.

Then again the next year.

She wasn't sure if he'd ever managed to graduate high school, as she'd been sent away from the Kramers' at that point.

Judging by his uniform, she supposed he must have.

Though given that his father was the walrus-shaped sheriff from the previous day, she wouldn't have been stunned if he hadn't. Nepotism wasn't just a good idea to most folk in Pinelake. It was considered something of a town custom.

"Ross," she said simply, nodding, willing her phone to connect. But Jamie didn't pick up. She lowered the device, checked the number, then tried again.

"Come over here," the big man said, glaring. His forehead was sweating already, though, he'd only made the exertion to rise from his vehicle. Ross Dawkins' partner was leaning against the hood now, frowning at Artemis. His eyes had narrowed into thin, mean lines behind his glasses.

"I—I have to be going," she said as politely as she could. She shot a look over her shoulder. A couple of other officers were lingering in the doorway, watching.

Though, perhaps *lingering* was generous. Blocking was more like it.

She started to move, walking away from the house, phone still to her ear, hurrying down the driveway.

"Hey!" Ross snapped. "Hey—I'm talking to you, civilian! Stop or you're under arrest!"

She hesitated, pausing, then glanced back. Jamie still wasn't answering her call. Another officer at the end of the driveway was staring now. None of the others said anything. They just watched.

She supposed she was the spectator sport of choice for the moment.

"I'm not sure you *can* arrest me, can you?" Artemis said, hesitantly. "Technically, I'm consulting with the FBI."

"Yeah right," Ross scoffed. "My dad told me about your little charade."

Artemis just watched him, her phone clutched delicately in her hand. He approached now, sauntering towards her, his thumbs tucked inside his shoulder holsters. The other locals didn't move.

Ross came to a halt in front of her. "Do you have an ID on you, citizen?"

She frowned. "Yes. But I'm not sure I have to give it to you."

She tried to slip by, but he held out a meaty hand, touching her shoulder and pushing her back a step. "Hang on," he snapped. "I didn't say you could leave."

She frowned at where his hand made contact. "Don't touch me," she said quietly, feeling her stomach churn.

"I need you to answer some questions," Ross said, scowling down at her.

She shot a look back towards the mansion doors, but the cops were still standing there, motionless but attentive. She clutched her phone in her hand, having once more gone to voicemail.

"What questions?" she said.

"You need to come with me," Ross said. He reached for her arm again, large fingers wrapping around her small wrist.

She tensed. Artemis had no desire to go anywhere with the thick-necked cop. She pulled at her arm, but the officer squeezed now, his fingers wrapped around her arm. "Stop resisting," he growled, beginning to reach for his handcuffs.

"Hang on, hang on," Artemis said, feeling a prickle along her cheeks. Whether it was a flush of embarrassment or rage, she couldn't really tell. "I'm consulting on the case—you saw me with Agent Grant. Your father saw me."

"We saw a serial killer's whelp come back to town..." he said, a sneer in his voice. "Right around the time women are being killed again. Coincidence?" He pulled the cuffs and began twisting Artemis' arm.

The man's small partner was standing off to the side, arms crossed, watching. Artemis didn't remember the faces of everyone watching, but she recognized most of them. The last time she'd been in town, she wondered if some of these uniformed onlookers had anything to do with the harassment she and Tommy had received while staying at the Kramers'.

Now, her heart pounded as her arm twisted. She knew with men like Ross, resistance only made them angrier. Compliance only made them more demanding.

"How come you're back in town?" Ross was muttering in her ear, his breath carrying the scent of beer and cigarettes. "How are you involved with this?"

She tried to speak, but suddenly, her phone began to ring.

She lifted it with one hand, answered hurriedly and said, "Hello, Supervising Agent Grant? Yes... I'm right outside. I'm afraid one of the police officers is attempting to arrest me." She said this pointedly, her words coming in a sudden rush.

Ross Dawkins' hand tensed on her arm. He tried to reach for the phone, but Artemis' jerked her head to the side. "You'd like to speak with him? Oh, the police chief? Alright—I'll let him now." She extended her phone towards Dawkins now, her eyebrows rising on her pale skin. "The Supervising Agent demands to speak with you. You better answer."

Of course, it wasn't Agent Grant on the phone. She hoped Ross couldn't pick out Jamie Kramer's confused comments. But she'd phrased the comment as a demand, and with men like this, she knew they liked issuing commands, never following them.

Dawkins stared at the phone, snorted, then with a disgusted mutter, gave her a little shove. Artemis stumbled back, still holding her phone. He pointed a meaty finger at her. "This is my town," he snapped. "Not yours. Not the FBI's. Mine. You guys answer to me."

"Isn't your grandfather the Sheriff?"

"Hell yeah. My father's the sergeant. My little brother's my partner." He pointed at the man leaning against the hood of the car. "And you," he snapped, "had better get the hell out of here. We don't want you here, Blythe. I mean it. Get the hell out. I don't care what bullshit the FBI is playing at. You're not welcome. Got it?"

Artemis swallowed but nodded a single time. "Understood," she said softly.

She didn't protest, didn't add anything else. For the moment, it seemed as if she'd been saved from an unpleasant trip down to a police station. She turned quickly and began hastening away, raising her phone as she did.

"Hello?" she murmured, feeling eyes watch her retreat. Her skin crawled under their scrutiny.

"I—Artemis?" Jamie's voice said, sounding extremely confused.

Artemis reached the end of the long driveway and only then, with a shaky breath, did she look back. Officer Dawkins was still staring at her, as were the other cops in the driveway. The looks of hatred, of contempt, of suspicion only propelled her onto the street. She began walking up the asphalt, moving in the direction of the Kramer residence.

As she walked, she realized her hand was trembling badly, her breath coming in short, frightened huffs. "I—I sorry, Jamie. Just…" Her voice shook with emotion. But Artemis didn't cry anymore… Didn't quite remember how. She continued her trek away from the Ortega residence. Even if she could have cried, she knew she didn't want to. This was all par for the course in Pinelake. At least this time they weren't throwing bricks through her bedroom window. She wouldn't cry.

Not with Jamie Kramer on the line.

"Hey, Artemis—so sorry. I'm actually heading to the office now to... to pick up some things." He sounded strange as he said it. In the background, she thought she heard a blare of a horn. "Shit," he said. "Could I call you back?"

"Umm, y-yes. Do you—"

"Tommy's number! Dammit. I knew I forgot something. Yes—I'll get my phone from the office too. Right away. So sorry, Artemis. Things have been... well..."

"Of course," she said quickly, wincing. "I'm so sorry. Of course. No... no rush."

Another blare of a horn in the background, a quick apology, then Jamie said, "Sorry, Artemis. Talk soon! Bye!"

He hung up.

She massaged her eyes, wondering if she had simply bitten off more than she could chew. Jamie had lost his mother. Her brother had a stupid ring that matched a mobster's description of a suspect, and now she'd agreed to go to the Elk Lodge just to get judged by a bunch of rich women.

She heard tires against tarmac and glanced sharply back to see Agent Forester pulling out of the driveway.

She let out a faint sigh of relief that it wasn't Ross or one of his colleagues.

She waited by the curb as Forester approached, rolling down the window and peering out at her.

"Hey there," he said, cheerful. "Need a ride?"

"Wish you'd asked five minutes ago," she muttered.

His smile faded. "What?"

"Nothing. It's fine." She steadied herself with an exhale, nodded and, circling the car to enter the passenger side, she waited until she'd opened the door and slipped into the car to say, "We're going to need your badge to get in."

"Sounds good. So where is this fancy-schmancy place?"

"Golf course," Artemis said. "South of the lake."

"A golf course. For real?"

"Things don't change in Pinelake, Agent Forester. Here, take the next left."

As she instructed Forester towards the Elk Lodge, Artemis felt her stomach twist. What if she was right about the book club? Was she putting herself in danger by heading there?

She shot a look at Forester. He seemed so at ease.

She wondered what it was like, not to really *fear* things.

She felt a jolt of envy.

She leaned back, frowning through the windshield.

Sometimes, it almost felt like everything short of her own shadow scared her. And in Pinelake, there was at least *one* thing lurking in the dark that warranted her fear.

18

Artemis shifted uncomfortably as she walked up the carved, wooden steps of naked logs treated in some type of see-through coating. Above, four sets of elk antlers spread like a chandelier over the stone-slab porch of the exclusive lodge. Beyond the wooden columns and stone base, she spotted long fields of green where golfers, in small carts, puttered around.

On the porch, through a glass window, around the side of the enormous lodge, she spotted figures in large bonnets, dresses, and more than one leather-bound bible.

"Is that the book club?" Forester asked, peering through the window.

"Bible study," Artemis replied. "Don't touch one of their books. I'm pretty sure it might scorch you."

"I see this place has got you a bit snarky."

Artemis shot Forester a long look, standing with one foot braced on the wooden steps. "It's not this place," she said with a frown. "It's you."

Inwardly, though, she was cursing *this place.*

Even as a kid, she'd never been allowed in the lodge. Membership fees alone were rumored to go higher than her family's rent had been. Even as a mentalist, a fleecer, her father had always been stingy with money. She'd never quite known how much he'd made.

Now, as she shot a look towards the parking lot filled with bright and shiny cars that looked more like rocketships than automobiles, she felt doubly certain that her plain sweater and dark trousers were going to stick out like a sore thumb.

Thankfully, she was accompanying a man who seemed to make a living as an even bigger thumb.

"Heya!" he said cheerfully, waving towards two older women with white curls who were pushing out of the front doors. They shot Forester a look, both smiled at him. One patted him on the wrist and the other reached into her purse and then slipped a one dollar bill into his hand. "Thank you, young man," she said in a creaking voice.

Then, the two women, adjusting the straps of their purses, slowly took the wooden stairs.

Artemis spotted a valet pulling what looked like a Bentley around the corner.

With the door open, Artemis caught it with her foot and gestured at Forester. "Come on," she said. "Try not to fall in love, alright?"

Forester glanced at the dollar, back at the ladies, then at Artemis. "What... what did I just get paid for?"

Artemis snorted. "Being tall, probably."

"Huh. That's a thing?"

"I mean... maybe if you linger around here you might find your true calling, Forester. Forget this FBI business, you could serve as geriatric eye-candy."

"Huh, well... on second thought," he muttered, "Maybe I'll leave this here."

He placed the dollar directly on the ground, then followed her through the doors.

A second set of doors with a buzzer blocked their progress. These were even more ornate than the first. No more elk antlers above the threshold, but instead, the door frame itself looked as if it were made from stained glass.

A man on the other side of the glass peered towards them. He wore a crimson uniform with a crimson cap.

"Hello?" the man's voice came over the speaker. "Do you have memberships?" He sounded seriously doubtful.

Artemis nodded at Forester. He raised his badge. "This count?"

The crimson-uniformed man hesitated. He paused. "I'm afraid I'll have to speak with someone. One moment."

And then he ducked out of sight.

Forester flipped his ID open and closed a couple of times, frowning. "Huh. Usually that works," he said.

"Maybe it's broken."

"See—there it is. Snark. And it hurts, Ms. Blythe. It hurts deeply."

Artemis snorted, shaking her head. She watched through the colored glass as the figure emerged a few seconds later, this time accompanied by another person. A woman's voice came over the speaker now.

"Hello, my name is Seema Hofster. How can I help you?"

Forester held up a finger towards Artemis, an expectant look on his face. Then, he flashed his badge again.

"FBI?" said the voice.

Forester closed the badge, nodding.

"Is there a problem?" the woman said, sounding somewhere between a concerned mother and a flight attendant. A practiced voice. A voice that made Artemis wince. She sighed and turned, glancing off through the first layer of doors now.

"We're here about a book club," Forester said.

"Oh... hmm. Do you know which one?"

Artemis turned. "They're reading *The Invisible Man*."

"I see..." The woman sighed. "I regret to inform you that this particular book club is currently on hiatus. I'm afraid there have been some health complications with—"

"Members are dead?" Forester cut in.

The woman on the other side of the glass let out a long exhale. "I... yes. I'm afraid so."

Forester glanced at Artemis, shrugged once. "No book club anymore," he murmured.

Artemis, though, said, "How many people were in the book club?"

"I'm afraid I'm not at liberty to divulge clients' personal information. If you come back with a warrant," the voice said evenly, "I'm sure we can discuss further."

"They might be in danger," Artemis replied slowly.

"Mhmm. Well... I can pass along a word. What would you like me to tell them?"

Forester was picking at his fingernails. "Oh. Dunno. Someone might hunt them in the privacy of their own homes and kill them in a gruesome manner." He shrugged. "But it's okay... FBI wanted to help but weren't allowed. Cuz no warrant."

He looked up again, peering through the glass.

The woman on the other side shifted uncomfortably, her features still mostly obscured by the colored material.

"Look," she said quietly, "I can't give you that information. I nearly lost my job last week for speaking with a non-member about this very subject. Now, please, if you'd like more, come back with a—"

"Hang on," Artemis cut in. "What non-member?"

"Pardon?"

"You said someone else was asking about the book club?"

"Umm, yes… a very angry man, actually. A non-member."

"So you *can* divulge information about him, can't you?"

"Y-yes…" the woman hesitated, and Artemis heard the distinct sound of swallowing over the speaker. "It… he was quiet angry, actually. He wanted to know about one of the women in the book club."

"And has anyone else asked about them? Does anyone have access to a membership list?"

"Well, unfortunately, as I said, the club has been on hiatus. For a few months now."

Artemis frowned. "Wait, *months*?"

"Yes. Months. I am aware of the recent slew of violence, but I assure you the book club was put on pause nearly four month ago. Apparently, some of the women couldn't agree over which book to read. It's—look, I don't see how this is relevant."

Artemis was frowning at Forester now. If the book club wasn't even *active* anymore, then could the killer still be targeting it? It seemed *less* likely… not impossible. But what was the motive? And how was it connected to the victims.

Artemis paused. Then she said, slowly, "Could you describe this irate man, please?"

"I... I suppose. Since he *was* a non-member," the disembodied voice over the speaker emphasized. "Handsome. Neat hair. Neat suit.. . I—actually, I believe he was related to one of the club members."

Artemis felt a faint prickle along her skin.

"Do you know which club member?" Forester asked, frowning.

"I'm not at liberty—"

"Right, right, forget I asked."

Forester shook his head in frustration. Artemis, though, felt a buzz along her skin.

A handsome man whose mother was in the book club?

She hated to even *think* it.

She thought of what the jeweler had said about a man with a ring asking about the gold two days after Mr. and Mrs. Kramer had purchased it from him.

Now that she thought of it... She frowned, her expression darkening. She was no longer sleep-deprived. No longer scatter-brained after her trip into Seattle with Forester.

Now, standing there, thinking clearly again... she pictured those rings on the horrible, poison-bloated fingers of Ms. Ortega.

She hadn't seen him wearing it in the garden...

But Tommy wasn't the only one with a junior varsity championship ring. Her brother and Jamie had known each other from playing football together. They'd won that championship on the same team.

Jamie *also* had a ring like that.

But so did the rest of the team that year. Fifteen years was a long time... but most people from Pinelake *stayed*. Others would still have their football rings as well.

She shot an uncomfortable look towards Forester, who was still speaking over the intercom, fishing for more information. Inevitably, Forester would also realize Jamie was a connection. Artemis needed to look into this herself, before getting anyone else involved.

She bit her lip, holding back a shout of frustration.

She knew what she had to do. And the first step didn't involve the FBI. Couldn't. She owed them that, didn't she?

If it turned out her brother or Jamie were involved... She wasn't sure her soul would survive it.

But she still owed them *something* for all those times spent in the woods together. The laughs, the joy... Happier times. The mountains were lonely places for some. But for Artemis, loneliness had only started when she *left* the mountains.

Then again.

Fifteen years was a very long time...

And people changed.

She forced a smile and held up a finger towards Forester, mouthing *one moment.* She indicated with her finger where she was headed then stepped through the sliding glass doors, back outside.

Forester shot her a look but didn't say anything as she hastily took the steps.

Her phone was back in her hand.

The number already dialing.

This time, traffic wouldn't be an acceptable excuse.

After the fourth ring, as she moved between gleaming cars in the parking lot, he answered.

"Hello?" Jamie's voice, a forced, over-the-top cheerfulness, suggesting he was irritated or upset and wanted to compensate.

"Jamie," she said, trying to sound equally affable. "Hey... you mentioned a meal last night. Look—would you mind meeting up? I still need to get that number from you, but I'd like to get brunch, if you'd like."

"Absolutely," he said, without hesitation. She could hear the excitement in his voice.

"Great!" she said, feeling a surge of her own anticipation which was quickly swallowed by a spurt of fear. Was Jamie involved? How could she know for sure?

"I was just about to text your brother's number. Sorry for the delay."

"No worries—and, one other thing," she said quickly. "This might sound weird, but do you have a yearbook from that year where you and my brother won the junior varsity football championship?"

"I..." He swallowed. "I think so. My mother was the one who..." He sighed. "I'll find it. Feeling nostalgic now that you're back in town?"

Artemis hesitated, bit her lip, but then said quietly, "Something like that. I'll see you soon! Where do you want to meet?" She decided not to mention the new victim. Not yet. Perhaps it would help her to keep some cards close to the vest.

Jamie paused then said. "You know, I think I might have the perfect spot in mind. I'll text and I'll look for that yearbook. See you in a bit, Artemis!"

Again, he sounded so excited.

She felt a flare of guilt as she hung up, her heart twisting. It didn't feel right; she so desperately wanted to enjoy what little allotment of reprieve she had from the bad blood in Pinelake. The FBI sniffing around, looking to her for a lead; she knew it was playing both sides to go off and investigate on her own. She needed a ride back from Forester, but she refused to tell him a thing. Not yet. She cared too much about Jamie, about Tommy. She couldn't just turn them over as names on a blank sheet to be investigated. No... no doing it this way was the right thing... At least, so she hoped. But she also had to remind herself, this wasn't a social call.

It was an interrogation.

One way or another, she would find out if Jamie was involved.

Because if he wasn't, that meant her twin brother was at the top of the suspect list.

<h1 style="text-align:center">19</h1>

Artemis moved up the trail behind the Kramer residence, and her insides were bubble wrap. Every few steps across the pine-needle strewn path accompanied a faint pop of anxiety. She glanced back towards the large Kramer mansion, a jolt of sadness accompanying her hesitant regard. She spotted Mr. Kramer, sitting in the backyard, staring up at the mountains. The older Kramer looked exhausted, rings under his eyes. He didn't notice her, his gaze vacant as he gazed over the freshly filled hole where his wife had been buried. Jamie had mentioned Mr. Kramer's health was failing, and he looked it. She'd never seen such sagging shoulders. A walking cane rested across one of his knees, and as he stared at his garden, he hung his head, his frail shoulders beginning to shake.

She felt a pang of pity. Jamie had mentioned his father still loved their mother... in his own way.

Artemis sighed, wondering if she ought to emerge from the tree line and comfort the old man. But he'd been the one who'd kicked her out when Tommy had run away. He'd been the one who'd given into the town's taunts and threats. Not that she blamed him. Not really.

But she didn't think he'd accept a comforting hand from her.

So she moved on as the old man sobbed quietly in his backyard. She wondered how many others in the surrounding area had wept the same way because of her own father.

The thought sent a chill along her spine, but the frigid sensation didn't last.

The air beneath the sun was warm now but cooled her skin from the occasional zephyr as she moved up the trail. So many memories of taking this path late at night, following the boys up the slopes. She could still picture Tommy, pausing every now and then to throw a pinecone or a rock at a squirrel. She had always been able to tell her twin brother's mood by what sort of projectile he chose for the woodland creatures.

She frowned, kicking a pinecone off the path as she hastened up the slopes. Jamie hadn't joined in with Tommy's cruelty to small critters. He'd protested right along with Artemis. It had become something of a secret mission for the two of them to note Tommy's mood and then make noises or wild gestures to scare of any animals before Tommy could start aiming.

She smiled at the memories. A bittersweet thought. Those hadn't exactly been *happy* times. Nothing in her life had been anything other than a mixture of both sadness and brief glimmers of sunlight.

She continued up the slopes, heading towards one of their favorite lookout spots. She double-checked her phone, reading the last message. *Just arrived—picnic ready. See you soon!*

She wanted to smile. Wanted to enjoy the thought of a secret picnic in the woods, their childhood stomping grounds. Jamie, waiting for her.

And yet now all she could feel was anxiety.

Was this a mistake? Was she walking into something... something dangerous.

"Shut up," she muttered to her own thoughts. She refused to think Jamie could ever harm her.

But then why had a jeweler spotted someone with his football ring enter the gold shop *after* the Kramers had purchased their new glinting investment? Who else also had a football ring?

This was why she'd asked Jamie to bring his yearbook. To go through the faces, the names.

It wasn't Jamie.

It wasn't Tommy.

She... she couldn't survive if another man in her life turned out to be a monster. She couldn't let it happen.

As she moved up the trail, beneath the shaking boughs, she spotted movement ahead from one of the old lookout spots. Tommy would often set off bottle-rockets nearby. Jamie had tried his first sip of beer on those slopes. Artemis had refused the alcohol at first but eventually given in. She'd never much acquired a taste for the stuff, though.

Along a faint line of grassy slope, she spotted where Jamie Kramer lingered, sitting cross-legged on the ground, his back pressed to a mossy stone beneath a much larger jutting wall of stone. A small, red-checkered blanket was placed beneath him, spread out across the ground where the grassy incline met stony shelf.

As she approached, her rising sense of anxiety slowed her footsteps. The large trees cast their shadows over her. The wilderness and slopes about her shielded them from prying eyes.

From witnesses, too.

Jamie Kramer was still sitting butterfly-legged, his sharp, attractive features silhouetted against the mountain. He worked out, she decided. People didn't manage *that* little body fat without working out. He was no longer wearing that banker-suit from before but instead wore a plain, blue t-shirt. She spotted the small corner of a tattoo beneath his left sleeve. Tommy and Jamie had both gotten those tattoos—each one half of a king's crown. They'd tried to convince Artemis to join them, but she'd been too afraid of needles.

She sighed. A lot in her life could be traced back to the fears she'd had as a child.

Now, though, she stared at the faint tattoo beneath Jamie's sleeve, approaching the makeshift picnic spot.

Jamie glanced over, his expression brightening. He stood quickly, dusting a few stray pine needles off his trousers. "Hey!" he said, beaming. "I wasn't sure how far you were."

Artemis' feet wanted to slow again. More fear, she realized. The same fear that had stopped her from getting a tattoo with her brother and Jamie. The same fear, though she didn't like thinking it, that so often kept her cooped up in a bedroom, or a small apartment, playing games online instead of facing the world.

Those games, though, had built her a career. Was starting to make her more money than she ever thought possible. Eventually, if she continued her winning streak, she'd be able to retire young.

But though her feet protested the forward momentum, the rest of her forced her body forward. She reached the edge of the red-checkered blanket. She glanced down, up, then couldn't help but smirk. "At least you got the blanket right."

Jamie followed her gaze. "What?" he said, sensing the teasing in her voice. "What's wrong? Oh—oh, the picnic basket?"

She snorted. "That's not a basket. Is that... a laundry hamper?"

Jamie chuckled, rubbing sheepishly at the back of his head. "I... mean..." he trailed off. "You might not like the lunch either."

She frowned, leaning over and peering into the white laundry basket. She hesitated, then let out a little snort of amusement. "Are those lunch-packs?"

"Yeah… Sophie had some left in the fridge. Do you want peanut butter and jelly breadsticks or cold salami and crackers?" Jamie was lowering again, sitting once more on the blanket.

As he dropped, Artemis stared at his fingers.

No ring. Had he taken it off? Had he stopped wearing it?

She remembered when Jamie and Tommy had first been given those rings—neither boy had removed them for months. And then… Tommy had done his vanishing act, and Artemis had left the Kramer home.

This wasn't the Jamie she remembered. She couldn't afford to forget that fact. His perfectly parted hair shifted only slightly in the mountain breeze. He watched her, a twinkle in his eyes.

She glanced back, standing on the edge of the checkered blanket, her knee brushing the edge of the laundry hamper he'd used for a picnic basket. She swallowed slowly, meeting those twinkling eyes.

"Everything alright?" he said softly, looking up at her. Then, he snapped his fingers. "Almost forgot. I brought that yearbook you asked for." He waved towards the basket, reached inside, moved about a couple of the school children lunch packs then emerged holding an old, brown yearbook with a few of the pages jutting out the top, hinting at a less than optimal binding.

He placed it on the blanket between them.

She could feel her emotions warring, feel her hand itching to reach for her phone. It wasn't too late to call Agent Grant, to tell Forester where she was. The two of them were still only a few houses up the street at Ms. Ortega's.

But as she looked at Jamie Kramer, she simply couldn't bring herself to do it.

So few of her memories were fond ones... especially after Helen was killed. She couldn't afford to rob herself of any more without first investigating her friend on her own.

And so, slowly, trying to hide her shaking fingers, she lowered to the blanket, swallowing as she did. The moment she sat, Jamie handed her one of the lunch packets. The plastic film had been pulled aside on this one. She frowned at the open container.

"Sorry," he said quickly, noticing her attention. "Just found it in the fridge like that. Sophie must have not liked it."

Artemis took the tray of peanut butter and jelly breadsticks. For one horrible moment, she wondered if perhaps anything had been *slipped* into the food. She lowered the tray onto the blanket.

"So," Jamie said, conversationally, "This is fun, huh?" His expression soured a bit as he removed the second tray of food and shifted the yearbook between them. "Been a while... what was it, like ten years?"

"Fifteen," she murmured back.

"Fifteen? Wow," Jamie just stared at her, watching her now. Neither of them touched the food. The forest around them seemed thicker now, darker. The sky above laden with cotton-white, threatening more shadows.

The breeze wasn't as warm up the slopes, through the trees. The scent of earth, of the forest, lingered on the air. Occasional glimpses of blue flowers amidst the undergrowth hinted at the source of more fragrant odors tinging the wind.

"I..." Artemis didn't know where to begin. She shifted uncomfortably, brushing aside some of her dark hair and watching Jamie.

He was staring at her, unblinking. Then, realizing he was staring, he quickly looked away and coughed delicately. "S-sorry," he said. "Sorry, didn't mean to... to... What do you think of your food?" he insisted, waving towards it.

She glanced at the corner of the plastic now fluttering with the wind. "Umm, I'm not that hungry."

"Come on," he teased. "I remember you always had an appetite." He was staring at her again.

A cold shiver trembled down her spine. She leaned back a bit, sitting cross-legged but wondering if perhaps she should have kept her feet. For the moment, though, Jamie was just watching her. No ring on his finger.

"Where's your ring?" she said suddenly, blurting the first thought that came to mind. She pointed.

"M-my... I'm not married," he said quickly. He swallowed, glancing off. "Lot of those people down there were, you know... Not anymore though. You can see for miles from here. Can see... everything."

She tried to stay on track. "I meant your old football ring."

"Oh," he said, laughing sheepishly and rubbing at his sculpted jaw. "Ha. Sorry, I guess... Just..." he was watching her again. "I forgot how beautiful they were."

"Excuse me?" her skin prickled.

He shook his head, forcefully looking away again. "Sorry—so sorry. Just..." he looked up, swallowing and then, in a far bolder tone, with no more stuttering, he said, "Your eyes. I forgot how beautiful they were... Like... like gemstones."

He didn't look away now. Didn't attempt anything close to "bashful." Briefly, it felt as if he'd intended the comment as a compliment. But a part of her wondered at this. All she could think of were the gemstones adorning the corpse in the bathtub back in the Ortega mansion. The gemstones in the jewelry of two of the victims.

Including his mother.

He wasn't acting like a man who'd lost his own mother. Had he meant it as a compliment? Or... or was it a more sinister comment? The breeze slowed now. The shifting grass impressed by the wind went still, perking up as if listening to the strange conversation on the slopes. The large, rocky outcrop above them jutted out like a terrace of stone, hiding the two of them in shadow.

Artemis spotted something else. She frowned, her eyes flicking towards the shelf of rock. Was that a plastic bottle jutting over the edge? She wrinkled her nose but looked back towards Jamie.

"Thank you," she said at last.

He gave a wry smile, a half shrug. "It's true," he said. "I've thought a lot about you, Artemis. Ever since you left."

I've thought about you, too. She wanted to reply. But instead, she said, "Where is it?"

"I—sorry, what?" He frowned now.

"Your football ring. Where is it?"

He wrinkled his nose, leaning back, his hands resting on his curled legs. "I'm... I'm not sure... Why are you so interested in my ring?"

"Just... just did you lose it, maybe?"

Inwardly, she was kicking herself. This was *not* a tactical gleaning of information without rousing suspicion. This wasn't a brilliant opening, masterfully engaging the first few moves of a strategic encounter.

This was a blunder. Full-speed and bumbling. She tried to rein herself in. "Just curious," she said. "I remember Tommy's ring. He loved it so much. I remember your tattoos as well."

Jamie seemed glad the subject had moved from his ring. He glanced at the edge of the tattoo beneath his shirt. Half an inked crown with a single gemstone in the center, cut off where the line faded. "Yeah," he said. "I remember you almost crying when Tommy tried to bully you into getting one also."

"I don't cry," she replied reflexively.

He hesitated. "Huh. Now that you mention it, I guess you don't."

"So where is it?"

"Where... the ring?" he crossed his arms now, wincing as he leaned back. She noticed he was favoring his left side.

What had the jeweler said? He'd punched the man in the ribs who'd come asking about the gold...

"Why do you care so much about my stupid, old football ring?" Jamie said, outright frowning now. The twinkle was gone from his eye. And once more, like everyone in Pinelake, he was watching a Blythe with nothing less than suspicion.

"I... I need to know, Jamie," she said, again realizing how tactless she was being. But she hadn't realized how much effect the forest, the isolation, would have. Hadn't thought she'd be *scared* sitting across from Jamie Kramer of all people.

"I don't know, Artemis," he said, somewhat coldly now. "I lost it. Or... or someone borrowed it. I haven't had it in years. I think I gave it to someone who asked me. It was a stupid, fake ring. Five dollar material, tops."

"You lost it?"

"Or loaned it," he replied quickly.

"But you don't remember who to?" She was pressing now. They both could tell she was pressing. He was scowling again. She felt shivers along her back.

"Why the hell does this matter so much to you?" Jamie retorted. "Also eat something." He waved more insistently to the packet on her lap. "Go on," he said. "You look starved, Artemis."

"No... no I'm fine. How about you eat this one?" She extended the package with the peeled corner to Jamie.

He glanced at it sharply and gave a quick shake of his head. "N-no. Just... These things actually give me indigestion." He gave a little nervous chuckle. And then suddenly pushed to his feet.

20

HE WINCED, RUBBING AT his ribs.

Artemis stared up at Jamie, the same prickle moving along her spine. She tensed where she sat on the blanket, watching Jamie Kramer closely. He *really* didn't seem broken up about his mother's death. And what were the odds he *lost* the very ring someone had spotted on their prime suspect? Maybe one of the local cops had warned Jamie they were looking for the rings. People in Pinelake could be somewhat insular.

Jamie shifted side to side, stretching his arms up, causing the hem of his shirt to lift.

She tried not to stare. At first, she noted the bottom line of a six-pack. She stared, trying not to look too interested. But she also noticed something else. Moving from the direction of the ribs, just on the other side of his belly button, a faint patch of blue and black... A thick bruise.

"What's that?" she said sharply, pushing to her own feet now and taking a quick step off the blanket.

"What?" he said, shooting her a confused look.

"Your ribs," she said. "Are—are they bruised?"

Instead of looking scared or alarmed, he just scowled. "Yeah. That tall numbskull you were with. I'm still thinking of pressing charges."

She thought of how Forester had thrown Jamie to the ground back at his place.

She let out a shaking sigh. A lost ring... a bruise in the same spot the jeweler had mentioned... a coldness towards his dead mother...

"Jamie," she said slowly, her voice creaking like the hinges of an old chest. "Were things *very* difficult with your mother?"

He frowned. "What?"

"I... just want to..."

Suddenly, his eyes widened. "Holy shit," he said, biting off each word. "Are you... you're not serious, are you?"

She winced. "Just... Please. What was between you two?"

"Shit, you are." He just gaped at her. "You're investigating me? You think I had something to do with this? My *own* mother!"

Subtlety clearly wasn't her strong suit in that moment. This wasn't at *all* like a chess match. Too many emotions involved. Her own included. Isolated, alone on the side of the mountain, her skin prickling, icy fingers probing down her neck. Sometimes, though, even if painful, sacrifices had to be made. She'd come here to clear Jamie's name. But now he was yelling at her. Not that she blamed him. She would have likely reacted the same way.

But he had bruised ribs. A missing ring. She wasn't sure why he kept insisting she eat the stupid lunch-pack. Why was the wrapper open? Was he... was he intending to hurt *her*?

The thought shocked her system. She nearly lost her footing, as her legs went weak.

"Jamie," she said quietly. "I have to know. You don't seem that broken up about your mother."

"You think I killed her," he said, his voice cold.

"No... No, I didn't say that. I'm just *asking*. I'm here on my own, Jamie."

"Alone, hmm?" he said, swallowing now. He shot a look down the trail, scanning the trees.

And suddenly, she wished she hadn't said this last part. She'd been hoping to let Jamie know she wasn't trying to get him in trouble. But now... what if he *was* involved? What if he was the killer?

What if she'd just told a serial killer that she was alone in the woods?

He stared at her... His eyes meeting hers. Eyes like gemstones—that's what he'd said. He shot another nervous look towards the trees. Was he searching for FBI? Fearful he was being watched...

Or was he looking for witnesses? Wondering if now was the best time to strike?

Jamie Kramer was handsome as ever. But was it the quiet, composed beauty of a kind, honest man? Or was it the sheer veneer of a psychopath like Ted Bundy?

His voice was shaking now as he spoke. Rage? Or fear. It was so hard to tell in that moment. Her mind was fritzing. Her usual ability to focus on emotion, on body language, was short-circuiting standing this close to Jamie. Attraction, terror, memories...

Her mind was in chaos. She'd made a mistake coming here. She knew that much.

"My mother and I were on the outs," snapped Jamie. "I told you that. She was *torturing* my old man. He's almost dead as it is. Cancer. Three years ago. He's almost gone."

"I... I'm so sorry. I didn't know."

He took a step towards her. She took a step back. He froze as if she'd slapped him. "You really think I did it?" he said, stunned. He stepped on the yearbook, but glanced down, frowning at it. "Why did you ask me to bring this?"

"Your ring," she said quickly, standing off the blanket on the pine needles now. "Someone went to the jeweler's store asking about the gold your mother and father purchased..." It took more courage than she thought she had to add this next line. "Was it you?"

He glared now, his eyes flashing. "Hell no! That's not how it happened anyway. The jeweler is lying!"

"He said he punched the man in the ribs. The one who came after. Said the man was wearing sunglasses and a hood."

Jamie was yelling now, his face turning red. "No hood. No sunglasses," he bellowed. He raised his fingers, all ten, wiggling them towards her. "No damn ring. So do you have any more accusations? Just because I'm not crying in public, doesn't mean I'm not crying, Artemis. You just said yourself—you don't cry. Maybe I learned it from you. Maybe they should investigate the Ghostkiller's daughter, huh? Maybe *you* killed my mother. I don't see you weeping!" He was yelling now, his tongue lashing her with shallow cuts.

She wasn't sure if this could have possibly gone worse. Her voice shook with emotion as she tried to keep herself composed. "I'm," she swallowed, "Not trying to hurt you, Jamie. I'm trying to help. I came alone because I don't want to believe it's you. But look at it from my perspective!"

He took another step towards her, but this time she stood her ground. He faced her, a bit taller, breathing heavily, glaring at her. He raised a hand, pointing at her face. "I missed you. I wanted to meet, because I missed you. Serves me right, I guess. This whole damn town is cursed. Ever since..." he shook his head, looking off with a haunted gaze. "Your damn family, Artemis. Your dad did this. Things haven't been the same. My old man dying. My mother dead. I'm living back at home—did they tell you that? Lost my job. Yeah, yeah look at me with pity. Poor Jamie Kramer, unemployed. Shit." He shook his head now, using the same hand he'd been pointing with to massage the bridge of his nose. "You think I killed my mother? Go talk to Sheriff Dawkins."

"Wh-why?" she said, her voice still shaky.

"Because!" he retorted. "Dawkins owns that car lot—I was interviewing to become a damn car salesman, Artemis. Not all of us are big shots now! I stayed in Pinelake. You left!"

"I didn't leave!" she yelled back suddenly, unable to keep her temper in check. "I was driven out of town! By your dad!"

"It wasn't my dad's idea—it was my mother's! She sent you away. She chased Tommy away, then sent you away. The only two things in my life that…" his voice cracked suddenly, and the prickling red across his cheeks now tinged his face. "That mattered…"

"I *didn't* ask to leave," Artemis retorted with gritted teeth. "I heard your parents arguing. Your father was the one who wanted me to leave."

"No…" he murmured softly. "No, it was my mother. She did that, Artemis. A lot. She was a manipulator. You don't know the half of it."

"What do you mean?"

He glared at her now, though. "You're the hotshot detective now. Figure it out. Talk to Sheriff Dawkins. I was with him when my mother was killed. The coroner confirmed it. No—I mean it. Now!" He snapped. He pointed at her pocket. "Take your damn phone out and call him."

"I believe you, Jamie," she said. She wished she meant it.

"I don't care! Take your phone out. Come on—you think I killed my own mother. So see if I'm lying. Call him! You won't, fine… Here. Let me! Christ, Artemis. I… I thought you…" he glanced at the picnic, back at her, then shook his head in frustration. He turned away from her now, marching towards the edge of the trail where the reception was best. His own phone was now in his hand. She watched him, her skin prickling, her mind and heart competing in some race.

It took a moment, but then Jamie was snapping into the phone, doing his best to keep his temper in check but failing. "Sheriff? Yeah, this is Jamie. Yes, sir. Look—I've got a..." he glanced at Artemis, eyes narrowed. "An FBI consultant here. They're asking me where I was the time of my mother's murder." Jamie snorted. "Yeah—I know it's ridiculous. Umm... yes... yes, it is her." Jamie hesitated, wincing. For a moment, he looked guilty. "I wouldn't say that, sir. She's..." he swallowed, scowling again. "Trying her best... I guess. Whatever. Could you tell her?"

Jamie gestured at Artemis. She stared at where he stood by the trail. Was this all a ploy too?

She didn't know what to believe. Her skin was crawling. She glanced off the edge of the cliff, staring across the many, large homes spread throughout the valley. She could see nearly everything from up here. She even spotted police moving about in Ms. Ortega's driveway. She thought she glimpsed the large, thick form of Officer Dawkins. The grandson of Sheriff Dawkins.

She let out a faint sigh. Then, slowly, wanting nothing more than to sprint off through the trees, she approached.

Jamie was still jutting the phone insistently in her direction. He'd turned it on speaker, and she could hear a voice on the other line now.

She drew nearer, frowning. Then a voice that shook with age, but still carried strength, snapped across the device. A voice of authority, a voice that reminded her of old plantation owners she'd read about from the seventeen hundreds. A no-nonsense, no mercy type of voice. Not quite a drill-instructor. Drill-instructors often communicated more bark than bite.

This voice... this voice carried both in equal and ample measure.

She recognized the voice, of course. One of the first voices she'd had to listen to when placed in that cold interrogation room at the age of fifteen. He hadn't stopped questioning her for hours. Had made her sleep in the cell. She didn't like the voice. But she at least knew who it belonged to.

"Sheriff Dawkins," she said quietly. "Yes?"

"Artemis Blythe?" the gruff voice barked.

"Yes, sir," she said, sighing and preparing to weather a storm.

She wasn't disappointed. "The gall on you, *girl,*" the Sheriff snapped. "To drag the good name of Jamie through the mud... For *you* of all people..." the voice trailed off, inhaling slowly. Artemis thought she heard a female voice in the background murmuring soothingly. She could picture Sheriff Dawkins' receptionist massaging the old, strong shoulders of the workhorse of a man.

More bad memories flitted back. Sheriff Dawkins had refused to do anything when the brick had been thrown through the Kramer window. Had refused to take seriously the threats made against Tommy. More than once, he'd arrested Tommy Blythe for smoking or loitering... things his own grandchildren and their friends did without reprisal. Ross and his gang had received a wink and a grin from patrolling officers.

Tommy had received handcuffs and a berating. More than one beating, too. Though he'd never ratted them out. Tommy had… taken revenge in *other* ways. She winced, remembering how her brother had once let loose a skunk in the Sheriff's own lakeside home.

"…was with me," the sheriff snapped. "Jamie Kramer was sitting in my office for four hours."

"Four hours for an interview about a salesman position?" Artemis said reflexively.

Jamie shifted uncomfortably on the pine needles. "Is that what he said?" the Sheriff scoffed. "It wasn't for no damn salesman position."

"What was it for?"

"None of your damn business. But he was here. My receptionist can tell you. Katie—here, tell the nosy Nelly who was in the office all afternoon."

"Hello?" a sweet, nervous voice said. "Hello, who is this?"

"Hello, Katie," Artemis replied with a sigh. Katie had been five grades below Artemis in school. She was nearly fifty years younger than the sheriff.

"I have the notes here," Katie said quickly in a meek but professional tone. "Jamie Kramer arrived at noon yesterday and left in a hurry at five-thirty."

"Five and a half hours?" Artemis said. She wrinkled her nose.

"The position he was interviewing for is an important one," snapped the sheriff. "But just so your smart ass understands. Jamie was here. Katie and I will both vouch for him as well as half the office. Got it?"

Artemis sighed. "Yes, sir."

She handed the phone back, expecting—and by the sound of things receiving—another berating she didn't want to listen to.

Jamie took the phone, wincing now. Some of his anger seemed to have receded. He was shooting uncomfortable glances towards Artemis. His eyes still held hurt, but then he shifted and winced from the pain in his ribs.

None of it made much sense to Artemis. Were the Sheriff and his receptionist *lying* for Jamie? Was his hatred for the Blythe family name clouding his judgment? Sheriff Dawkins wasn't a particularly fair man. But he was as hard as iron. Anyone... even his own wife... if caught committing a serious crime would be prosecuted to the fullest extent he could manage.

If he thought Jamie was involved, the Sheriff would throw him to the wolves.

Which meant...

It was more likely than not that the Sheriff was telling the truth. Jamie was in the man's office when Mrs. Kramer was killed.

Artemis let out a faint sigh of relief, feeling a sudden flush of gratitude. Jamie still looked angry and sad, refusing to glance in her direction as he bid his farewell then hung up.

Jamie didn't clean up the picnic. Didn't even look back. He said, "Here's your brother's number. He still wears his football ring. Maybe you should ask him." And then, he turned on his heel and marched back down the trail.

As he left, Artemis' phone buzzed.

She glanced down at a text from Jamie.

Tommy's number.

She felt a cold prickle along her spine.

Things couldn't possibly have gone worse.

But if the Sheriff was vouching for him...

It only left one suspect. She frowned, turning to quickly pick up the abandoned yearbook. Others had the same ring as Jamie. But only Tommy had the connection to the mob jeweler. She was ignoring the inevitable.

The way Sheriff Dawkins overlooked Ross's shortcomings but had hounded Tommy made her angry.

But was she doing the same? Ignoring all the arrows pointing directly to her own flesh and blood?

Some said... sociopathy was hereditary. Had her father's evil been inherited by her brother?

She scowled at this thought.

No... No, Tommy had his problems, but he wasn't evil. She refused to believe it.

Still... She hefted the yearbook and set off down the trail as well. Jamie was thankfully far enough ahead she didn't spot him now. She would speak to Tommy.

That was all. The yearbook... She'd give it to Grant and Forester. A lead, she'd say. It would buy her some more time.

As she moved away, down the trail, though, a faint chill crept along her back. She frowned, glancing back towards the overlook, the tall terrace of stone.

For a moment... it had almost felt like someone was watching her.

She shivered, hastening down the trail and picking up her pace, the yearbook tucked beneath her arm.

21

He watched through the trees, failing to hold back a frown. The creek ran at his feet, whispering where it grazed the muddy bank, swishing down the mountain slopes.

Jamie Kramer and Artemis Blythe moving down the mountain slopes, just like old times.

And yet they were both scowling, both fiddling with their phones.

He hated phones. But far more importantly, he hated the way Ms. Blythe was tampering where she didn't belong. He'd overheard parts of the conversation—he'd arrived late. But listening, he'd picked up enough.

Artemis Blythe was consulting for the FBI.

He let out a little sigh. Just like her old man had said she would. Of course... his conversation with the imprisoned Blythe had been surprising at first, but the Ghostkiller had been *more* than accommo dating… but for all the help, all the advice, the experienced serial killer had one, small request.

The source of the request was currently moving down the mountain trail, scowling after Jamie and switching her glare to her phone, exuding frustration.

By the sound of things, she'd suspected Jamie Kramer… Not that she was far off, was she?

He smirked now, allowing the frown to slip.

Today was a happy day.

Little Jamie wasn't so little anymore. Wasn't so… *innocent* either. But now things had changed. He'd been planning on waiting a day, letting the police disperse.

The next house call was across the street from Ortega's.

But now… with little Ms. Meddler and her troupe of nosy neighbors… perhaps it was time to expedite things.

He nodded to himself, shifting from one foot to the next, frowning at where Artemis Blythe disappeared through the trees.

She hadn't seen him. Hadn't known she had an audience.

They never really did, did they?

And his next job?

She wouldn't see it coming either. He'd glimpsed her staring through those large, front windows of hers, red and blue lights reflecting off the glass as she gaped across the street.

It was time she learned a lesson about being nosy.

The Ghostkiller had asked him to deal with Artemis Blythe. But first things first.

He had his own mission.

And this time, he wasn't going to be *nearly* so gentle.

He turned, stalking back down the trails only he knew on the mountain slopes, moving softly in the forest.

22

It had taken her five calls to reach Tommy, and then only in response to her third voicemail. Instead of calling back, he had simply left an address.

When she had looked up the location on her phone, she had wondered if he'd been teasing.

Now, as she pulled to a stop outside the abandoned train station, she wondered if she was being led into a trap. Was this really Tommy's number? Or was Jamie setting her up?

She sat in the back of the taxi, one arm braced against the window, the chill of the glass causing goosebumps to rise on her skin.

The taxi driver kept the meter running and kept glancing into the mirror, as if waiting for her to leave. But all Artemis could do was stare at the strange train station. Large, rusted walls made of corrugated metal cut the station off from the rest of civilization. An old, rundown industrial district served as the graveyard for the address she'd been provided.

"Are you sure this is it?" The taxi driver said slowly, glancing past her.

Artemis looked back at her phone. She held up a finger and called the number Jamie had provided once more. Her fingers tapped against her leg. The scent of stale smoke lingered in the air of the cramped car. Her window was jammed, making it impossible to air out the back seat.

She wanted to get out of the taxi, but even more, she wanted to avoid the strange, dilapidated space beyond.

Again, no one answered the phone.

She let out a faint huff of frustration. Again, she wondered if she was far more stupid than she thought. People online sang praises about her intelligence. Some of them spoke of her skill at chess in honorific terms that made her blush. But right now, she didn't feel very clever at all. She could still feel that strange chill, standing in the woods, facing Jamie Kramer.

Could still feel the icy sensation as she had stared into his eyes. The sudden sense of terror at the anger he had displayed. The tongue lashing she had received from Sheriff Dawkins.

She didn't know what to believe. But Jamie had a missing ring. Jamie had bruises on his ribs. Jamie clearly had some animosity towards his mother—he'd been acting strangely on the mountainside. The sheriff had vouched for him, though. She knew, after this conversation with Tommy, she might very well have to get the FBI involved. She had been thinking about this on the drive over. She didn't see any way around it. Someone was killing women. They weren't going to stop unless someone did it for them.

Her father had done the same. No one had seen it. No one had wanted to. Not even Artemis, or Helen, or Tommy. They had lived with the psychopathic killer and hadn't noticed a thing.

She shivered, remembering the first time she had read an article about what her father had done to those women. She bunched her fist and gave a quick nod of gratitude to the driver, paid him, pushed out the door, and stepped towards the rusted metal fence. The taxi driver lingered for a moment, as if wondering whether he should stay or not, but then the brake lights flashed red, and he moved back onto the road, circling past a chain-link fence, and picking up speed as he rushed away from the old, abandoned train station.

The air tasted strange. As if it coated her tongue with dust. Everything around her was orange, gray, or somewhere in between. Everything old, dying, broken down. Across the street, beyond the chain-link fence, she spotted a rusted tanker, and a truck without wheels. Further down, she spotted an old scrapyard.

She tried her brother's number again. And again, received no response.

She muttered darkly to herself, but then, with a sigh, she approached the metal fence.

Caution and warning signs adorned the surface. Threats of prosecution for trespassers or metal thieves also glared at her from behind laminated signs.

Someone had made markings on the signs, drawing crude cartoons, or declaring exactly what they thought of the police in less than complimentary terms.

"Tommy?" she called, shifting uncomfortably as she did. Part of her wished she had taken Forester up on that offer of a weapon. Part of her wished she had the tall agent with her. If this was a trap, she would need backup.

Why wasn't Tommy answering his damn phone.

She peered at the fence, glancing towards the main gate. Ajar—a rusted chain looping through two steel bars. But the chain was loose, and as she stepped towards it, her fingers trailed against the grainy surface of the metal bar. The gate emitted a low, creaking noise. Much of the dust and rust had already been shaken free, judging by scattered piles across the ground, suggesting people had used this entrance recently.

She pulled, widening the gap in the gate. The chain rattled, brushing against her fingers. Her hands were meant for clicking buttons or moving pieces. This was far outside the comfort zone. Why had Tommy given her this address?

She paused again, one hand prying open the gate, and her brow furrowing.

A mistake. This was a mistake. Everything about her instincts, on high alert, were warning her. Perhaps the best thing she could do for her brother was to give him the chance to meet up in a more public location. If, indeed, the number she had been given was for Tommy.

She hated this. Hated the mistrust. Hated the suspicion. Only hours ago she had been thinking about kissing Jamie Kramer. And now, she was wondering if he had tried to drug her with a lunch pack and then sent her into a trap.

She stood outside the rusted gate and reached a decision. Tommy would have to meet her halfway.

She was doing this on his behalf anyway, wasn't she?

She scowled at the thought, feet scattering dust and rust as she turned back towards the old road. If Tommy didn't reply this time, she would call a cab, head back to Pinelake and then…

She swallowed, considering it. She nodded firmly, though.

Then she'd tell Forester and Grant.

What other choice did she have?

She refused to set foot in some old, abandoned train station without backup. Already, she was living precariously by even *coming* here.

She nodded again, if only to affirm her own thoughts. Her phone was back in her hand. Carefully, not wanting to scare her brother, she texted.

Tommy, you should have recognized my voice. This is Art. Please reply. I'm at the location you sent. Where are you?

She hit send.

Then waited, frowning at her phone. The blank, glowing screen might easily have been a riveting World's match given the intensity she stared with.

But as the seconds ticked by, the minutes followed...

No response.

"Dammit, Tommy," she muttered beneath her breath.

Why was she here? What did she think she could accomplish? She tried to review the facts as dispassionately as possible.

Jamie Kramer had been given the lead on gold *by* Tommy. Tommy had a ring like the one Jamie did. Tommy was the son of a serial killer. Had he inherited more than just his father's last name?

Artemis hated thinking like this.

But...

She knew how the FBI would see it.

That was why she'd come.

To give her brother a fighting chance. No one had ever given Tommy a damn chance.

"Come on," she repeated, shaking her phone as if somehow this would help.

But still no reply.

She let out a faint sigh, beginning to turn to face the street again.

A taxi. She'd call a taxi again.

It wasn't her fault, was it? Tommy wasn't replying. What possible reason did her brother have not to—

A sudden screech of tires. A plume of dust.

She hesitated, frowning. And then, she stared down the road, stunned, as vehicles moved hastily towards her. Her heart hammered.

The taxi?

No... No, not the taxi.

A sedan... more than one shadow sitting in the seats. The dust made it hard to discern... but a car filled with men was hastening towards her.

And ahead of them, leading the charge...

A man on a motorcycle in black leather.

She swallowed, feeling her skin prickle. But only a few seconds later did she realize the truth...

The motorcycle wasn't *leading* them. The motorcycle was being chased. She glimpsed a flash of light from the front seat. And then, suddenly—

Taptap. Taptaptap.

She frowned. The sound of hailstones... of...

Her eyes widened and she suddenly flung herself back towards the gate.

Gunfire. The men in the sedan were shooting at the motorcyclist. She scrambled back, her spine pressing against the cold metal. More gunshots reverberated in the air. The two vehicles were now screaming towards her, dust flying, engines roaring, tires screeching.

The motorcyclist had music blaring from his vehicle: heavy metal by the sound of things. A cacophony of angry guitars and drumbeats like a rainstorm. A voice screamed into a microphone, emanating from the speakers attached to the motorcycle.

The biker had a thick, black helmet. The visor tinted. He wore black leathers, with a giant red skull stitched across his chest. He wore fingerless gloves, but now, two fingers, one on each hand, were being raised to the sky.

For a moment, he had removed his hands from the handlebars, choosing instead to flash the bird towards the man shooting at him.

Artemis just stared.

The reunion with her baby brother wasn't as nostalgic as she had hoped.

Of course, this was Tommy.

She would have recognized him even without that stupid red skeleton across the front of his clothing. Or that earsplitting music blaring from his motorcycle.

Then again, the easiest way to identify her brother was by the fact that someone clearly wanted him dead.

More gunshots.

Artemis wasn't versed in moments like these. She tried to think like Agent Forester. But his only advice when they had been shot at was to duck and run.

Her brother was currently doing just this, fleeing in her direction.

But the sedan, with the gunmen, didn't look ready to give up the chase.

She let out a shout of frustration, and then again worked furiously at the chain on the gate. If she opened the gate wide enough for the motorcycle, perhaps she could direct her brother to safety while keeping the sedan away.

Cursing Tommy under her breath and remembering vaguely why it had taken her so long to reconnect, she began twisting and yanking at the rusted chain. But it didn't budge.

More gunfire behind her, the metal music had reached a crescendo.

Cursing, she glanced frantically about. No stones, nothing to use—

There! Just inside the gate, a large, cement cinder block.

But it was too far out of reach.

She exhaled deeply, emptying her lungs, and then tried to slip through the gap between the metal gates. She ducked under the rusted chain, feeling the coarse way the links rubbed against her skull.

Her fingers found air. She strained, her chest aching, her back rubbing against coarse bar. She thought she felt something rip in the fabric of her shirt. Her fingers touched the very lip of the cinder block. She scraped, but missed. With another heave, groaning, she jammed her arm as far as it would go. Something strained. She thought, briefly, she might dislocate her shoulder. She let out a shout of exertion, and then her fingers hooked the oval gap of the cinder block.

She needed it. She could use it to smash the chain, to open the gate, and give her brother an escape route.

Her shoulder ached now from the exertion. She tried again, putting her whole body into it. Again, she felt her socket threaten to pop. Her shirt strained. Her chest would bruise, she felt certain.

Again, she hooked the cement block.

This time, painstakingly, she dragged it across the dust, towards the gap in the gate.

The chain above her head continued to rub her scalp raw. Now, the metal music was sweeping past her.

She cursed. Too slow. She didn't have time to open the gate. She managed to pull the block out. She lifted it, wanting to smash the chain. But the motorcycle was surging past her.

As it did, one of the hands, instead of flipping off the car behind him, waved towards Artemis in greeting.

She muttered darkly.

The sedan behind the motorcyclist kept coming. The man inside it didn't even seem to notice her in the cloud of dust picked up by their vehicles. They were still shouting, pointing in the direction of Tommy's bike.

One of the men poked his head out the window, shouting, aiming.

And so she did the only thing she could think of.

The motorcycle had passed. Smashing the chain wasn't an option.

A windshield, though?

Even Artemis had good enough aim to hit a windshield with a thick brick.

She winced, hefted the thing, and then flung it as the sedan rushed by.

The brick didn't go nearly as far as she had intended.

It wasn't like she spent her spare time hefting building materials for fun. Instead, the brick missed the windshield and went straight through the passenger side window.

She winced, yelping a warning.

She didn't see what the cinder block hit. But by the sudden shout and then silence, she guessed it had struck one of the gunmen.

And in turn, the gunmen, she guessed, must have hit the driver.

Because as the sedan sped past, the brick entered the window, the gunmen failed to take a shot, the vehicle suddenly skidded. The wheel spun, dust picked up as brake lights flashed angrily at her.

Once, twice, swerving left then right, trying to correct the sudden change in momentum, the vehicle failed to stay on the road. She stared, horrified, as the sedan slammed into the chain-link fence. It tore straight through. It only stopped moving when it hit the rusted truck within.

A *slam*. An instantaneous and loud scraping, grinding sound. Then silence.

The sound of impact faded, and her heart replaced the noise with loud pounding.

"Dear God, what did I just do?" she muttered to herself.

23

Artemis stared, bug-eyed, as figures began to move from inside the vehicle. Shattered glass scattered the tarmac. One hand jutted out the window *slapping* against the rusted metal of the tireless trick. Groaning voices, movements.

And then, a hand with a gun began pointing through the window, waving shakily but slowly leveling in her direction.

Her eyes widened. Her fingers still buzzed from the pressure of gripping that cinder block. She began to move but then heard a sudden rattle. A shift of chain as the rusted links were yanked through the gate like a snake.

And an arm shot out, grabbed her and pulled her roughly into the abandoned trainyard.

She yelped, protesting the treatment, but the man on the other end of that arm wasn't so much *strong* as determined. Wiry, she believed they called it.

Spluttering, desperate, she watched as a figure in a motorcycle helmet slipped the chain back between the bars, clicked a padlock in place, and then beckoned at her with spindly fingers just past those fingerless gloves. The same sort of fingers one might expect to find on a pick-pocket or lock-picker.

Her brother had moonlighted as both these things.

Now, he held one pale finger to his tinted helmet, hovering in an approximation of the location of his lips. He made a shushing sound and gestured for her to follow again, more insistently.

She wanted to protest, but now she could hear angry voices. More glass scattering, the sound of aching metal.

She couldn't see much through the small gap in the metal gate.

"Tommy!" she said, her voice fierce.

The figure in the helmet watched her, his face completely hidden. Then, true to form, he didn't say much. Just a quick, "C'mon." And he began to walk away, indifferent it seemed, if she followed or not.

She scowled after the man. He didn't have to remove that stupid helmet. The black leathers, the metal music blaring while flashing his middle-fingers towards men attempting to shoot him was clue enough.

Now, also, the wiry frame. Thin, scrawny some had called him. Tattoos were visible along the edges of his black, jacket sleeves.

He was sauntering away, though, and—deciding as much as she was furious with Tommy, she didn't want to linger and chat with their new friends on the road—she followed.

She continued to snap at him as he led her along old, dusty train tracks. Most the metal missing, likely repurposed or stripped. Wooden, rotten beams and ties were left in place. A couple of old, moldered boxcars were sun-stained and weather worn. An engine, toppled on its side, with pieces missing, was propped against an elevated, concrete platform overgrown with ivy and moss and clover.

"Tommy!" she insisted, quietly. "We need to get out of here! Come on. Where's your bike?"

But again, he didn't reply. Instead, he led her straight towards the toppled locomotive.

She tried to grab at his arm, but he yanked it away. He'd never been easy to control. Never been one to listen to input either. In fact, of the three Blythe children, Tommy had been the *least* enamored with their father.

At the time, Helen and Artemis had thought him a stick in the mud.

Now...

She wished she'd listened.

"Tommy," Artemis insisted. "Slow down. We can't stay here. They'll find us."

He paused, glancing back. "Won't," he said simply.

"Will!" she retorted.

He shook his head. "Nah. Too dumb. Come on. In here."

"Too... too dumb? Tommy that's *not* a plan! That's an assumption. Where are we going—dammit?"

Tommy clambered onto the concrete platform, flipped a metal door, like a hatch, and then dangled his legs into the dark. He paused long enough to peer down at Artemis where she stood on the dusty ground, amidst broken, wooden boards. He lifted his visor now, pulled his helmet off.

She met a familiar gaze. Mismatched eyes—one the color of wheat-fields, the other the hue of mountain streams. His eye colors were opposite to hers, just like so many other things different between the two of them.

He stared down at her with those familiar eyes. He now, she noted, had a stupid face tattoo.

She scowled at the two words etched along his neck, under his chin and reaching to his ears. They were in a language she didn't understand, and the ink was fading somewhat, suggesting it was an old tattoo.

He had a single teardrop ink stain in the corner of one eye. His hair was long, pulled back in a ponytail which had been shoved into the back of his jacket. His lips were pressed in a thin line, much in the way hers so often did when studying a complex problem.

He looked at her, didn't smile. Tommy rarely smiled. Then, curt as ever, he said, "Hey sis. Feel free to drop in."

And he did exactly that, dropping through the hatch of the sideways train engine, and disappearing into the dark.

Artemis wanted to scream. She stared at where her brother had vanished. Her frustration, as a sister, was quickly overshadowing the questions she'd rehearsed on the drive over. She hadn't even checked his fingers for the old football ring.

"Gah," she muttered, which wasn't a word, but it was the right thing to say in that moment. She scuffed her foot against one of the mealy boards, turning the soggy thing to splinters. She could hear voices, shouting. The sound of an engine attempting to start.

And then... she spotted knuckles on top of the corrugated fence. Her eyes bugged in horror.

She heard grunting, the knuckles shifting as, by the *clanging* sounds, it seemed as if one of the gunmen was attempting to scale the fence.

Heart in her throat, with nowhere left to go, she took the two metal rungs on the side of the engine her brother had, scrambled onto the top of the train.

Her eyes darted once more to the figures struggling to mount the gate. A second set of hands had joined the first. These bleeding, the fingers stained red. She heard cursing—speaking Spanish by the sound of things.

So far, though, no one spotted her. She winced and shot a final glance towards the dark hole in the side of the toppled engine. The yawning darkness seemed just as much a threat as the figures on the fence.

She glimpsed jutting, spiky black hair following the fingers, more grunting and faint shouting, suggesting now the two men were being helped from behind.

Too dumb. She thought to herself. What a theory. She bit her lip, dangled her legs into the darkness, feeling very much like she was about to go skinny dipping with sharks.

And then she dropped into the opening with a faint, frightened yelp.

24

As SHE STRUCK THE ground, nearly stumbling, it took her a second to reorient. She heard a faint *click* as the hatch above was swung back into place, aided by a pulley and a metal chain.

Her brother was standing with one arm raised, adjusting the cord in a groove by the trapdoor. Then, he turned to her.

"Tommy," she began, breathing heavily.

But he walked right past her, shoulder brushing shoulder, approaching a set of monitors in the wall. The train was toppled, but the room itself had been set up... sideways. So it felt right-side-up.

The monitors on the wall displayed feeds from close circuit cameras. Tommy watched with some interest as figures moved about in the train-station, keeping low and muttering to themselves.

"Tommy," Artemis whispered, "This is *not* a plan. Psst. *Tommy.*"

He glanced at her, held her gaze for a moment. Then blinked. And then he turned back to the monitors.

She scowled. "Really? Are you serious? The silent treatment? What are you, six? Come on—I need to talk to you about something. We need to get out of here. Where's your motorcycle?"

"Hid it," he said.

"Hid it, where? Can we get it before they find us?"

"Not gonna find us, Art," he replied with a grunt. He glanced at the CCTV monitors, then snorted. It was *like* a laugh but not *very* like one. He didn't smile. His eyes didn't twinkle. But as he watched the monitors, one of the men tripped on a tarp and hit the ground with a howl of fear. Another man nearly shot the screaming fellow by accident.

"Jumpy," Tommy muttered.

"Yeah, I bet," she said, glaring still. She tried to speak quietly, but her anger was rising. She grabbed at her brother's arm. "We need to *leave.*" But as she said it, she stared at one of the monitors.

Now... two men were walking on the platform *right next to* the toppled engine.

She went quiet, frozen in place. Her brother just watched, his expression more curious than anything. He crossed his arms, the red skull on his jacket rippling with the motion.

Artemis stared, frozen in place, fear prickling up her spine.

Tommy, bored, turned and began to make eggs.

A small refrigerator opened, a carton removed, he pulled a couple of white ovals and cracked them, pouring the contents on a skillet he had left on a small, propane stove.

He turned on the flame then reached for a spatula.

All the while, the men with guns crept along the top of the train, murmuring to each other and pointing one way or the other.

Typical Tommy. She had always suspected he might die on a gamble. For years, she had hoped to avoid being with him when that happened.

One of the men hesitated by the hatch, frowning. Above, Artemis could hear the sound of footsteps on the metal.

On the monitor, she watched as the man with the gun pointed towards the hatch.

Tommy, flipping eggs with one hand, reached into his pocket with the other.

He dialed a number, waited a moment, and Artemis looked desperately around for something resembling a weapon.

The small space in the sideways train engine had been turned into something of a bedroom. More like a creative homeless man's version of a bedroom. A pile of cardboard served as the main piece of furniture. There were strange metal protrusions in boxes that didn't make sense unless she tilted her head sideways to discern what they were. The few storage compartments, now sideways, served as useless openings on the ceiling, gaping down. The footsteps stopped, and one of the men was reaching for a handle on the trapdoor.

Her brother completed his phone call and slipped the device back in his pocket.

A few seconds passed.

And then a sudden explosion shook their temporary residence.

Artemis stared, eyes wide, at the CCTV. The men on top of the train stumbled, shouting now and pointing off in the distance.

Another man, visible on one of the other monitors, was sprinting, moving back towards the gate, flinging himself up the fence and clambering back towards the road.

Artemis wondered which one she had hit with the brick. Or, perhaps, if one of the men was still in the totaled car.

This thought was deeply unsettling.

Tommy paused, finagling with the eggs. He glanced at the monitors. "Over-easy? Scrambled?"

"What?" she snapped.

"Your eggs," he said, indicating with the spatula.

"What was that explosion?"

"Motorbike."

She stared at him. "You rigged your motorbike?"

He shook his head. "I rigged Pedro's motorbike."

"Who's Pedro?"

Tommy pointed at one of the monitors, sending a bit of egg yolk streaking the glass. "Bandanna, angry. Hand bleeding."

Artemis spotted the indicated man, who was now scrambling over the fence, and racing in the direction of a plume of smoke just visible on the corner of the screen.

"Why did you rig Pedro's motorbike?"

"Distraction."

She stared at her brother. "You were *riding* it, Tommy. Are you saying you were riding a motorcycle with plastic explosives strapped to the engine?"

He looked at her as if impressed that she knew what plastic explosives were. "Yup. Scrambled?"

"I don't want your stupid eggs."

He shrugged and began scrambling both the yolks, reaching for a plate now.

She resisted the urge to tug his ponytail like she'd use to. She could see the ink from those two-face tattoos just past his jawline.

Now there was no further motion on the monitors. She thought, vaguely, in the distance she could hear sirens.

She let out a faint, fluttering sigh. And that's when her eyes landed on her brother's gloved hand. Bulging on one of the fingers, visible just past the edge of the fingerless gloves, she noted a red piece of glass. She leaned in and quickly pulled back the edge of the glove.

It was the football ring.

He yanked his hand away, scowling at her.

She stumbled back, glaring but then cursing as she nearly stepped in a metal bucket with a couple of beers floating in what appeared to be, judging by the condensation, a bucket of melted ice. Only then did she realize just how chilly it was in here. But most of her shivers had nothing to do with the temperature.

"You... you're still wearing that thing?" she said stiffly.

He glanced at where her trembling finger pointed, then looked up. He didn't reply. He just stood by the propane stove, watching her.

"T-tommy," she said hesitantly, breathing in shallow huffs. "I know it's been a while."

"Fifteen years," he cut in.

"Yes... yes, *quite* a while."

"Fifteen years," he repeated more firmly.

She let out a sigh and rubbed at her nose. "Tommy, we can talk about all that later... I need to know something. Did you..." she swallowed. "Did you go to that jeweler friend of yours and ask about the Kramer family's gold purchase?"

He stared at her, his mismatched eyes flashing. Then he turned, snatched some of the egg out of the still hot skillet and jammed the food in his mouth with his bare fingers. The same spindly, scarred fingers that had been saluting the gunmen just a few minutes ago.

"Tommy," she murmured, "I... need to know if you..."

"How do you know 'bout the gold?"

She shifted uncomfortably. "Just... Jamie told me."

He looked back at her, nodding. "That why you back? Kramer?"

"Umm. Not exactly. It's a long story."

"Mhmm." He finished off the eggs, tossed the pan into a sink already piled high with dirty dishes and then moved over towards the padded cardboard boxes on the floor. He sat slowly, crossing his long arms over his knees and looking at her with a piercing gaze. "Why you back?"

"I told you, it's a long story."

"Nah. Ain't. People say that to dodge. So why?"

She could feel a familiar sense of irritation at her baby brother. Granted, she was only an hour older than him. But he never was able to drop a matter. The creased ridge of his brow line communicated all shapes of stubborn. She could remember him nagging Helen in the same way when they had been children. Nagging their father. Teachers.

Tommy had never been good at letting things go.

But this wasn't the child she remembered. He was now a thirty-year-old man who had connections to a serial murder.

She wanted badly to be wrong about her brother.

So she said, quietly, "FBI asked me to come."

He stared at her, and for the first time, her words seemed to have an effect. He tensed, frowning.

"They wanted my help on a recent series of murders."

He frowned now, nodding slowly. "Mrs. Kramer?"

"Among others. So you heard about her."

"Hard not to. Jamie is still in touch. He told me you were looking for me."

"And why did he tell you that?"

"Because you were looking for me."

"What are you and Jamie up to?" she blurted out. She was studying her brother's body language. Defensive, one foot tapping uncomfortably. But she knew better than to look too closely. He had been brought up by the same man. The Ghostkiller had taught his children how to read subtle cues but also how to disguise their own.

Tommy had never been the best at reading others. But he had been the best at hiding his own thoughts and emotions, even when left unspoken.

"Jamie is an old friend," Tommy said simply. "I'm helping him."

"By putting him in contact with the mob?"

"Who said anything about the mob?"

"Tommy! Stop it. Be serious. This is—"

"Is what? What is it? Why are you here?" Tommy shoved to his feet now, glaring at her across the toppled train car. "You don't call, you don't write. You don't visit. I almost forgot I had a sister."

Artemis scowled, her foot shifting nervously against the floor. She retorted, "Phones go both ways. Unless you didn't know that."

"You keep dodging. Which means I must've done something."

She stared at him. "Are you denying it?"

"No. I do a lot of things. Most of them illegal. Why is the FBI working with you?"

"That's not important. Tommy, I hate asking you, but where were you over the last couple of days? Do you have an alibi?"

The red skull on his leather jacket rippled as he crossed his arms again and said, "An *alibi*? That escalated." He was being cold, sarcastic now. The way he always got when he felt pressured into a corner.

"I'm trying to help you; I came alone. But Tommy, a jeweler spotted someone with your ring asking about Mrs. Kramer's gold."

"Jamie has a ring."

"He said the same thing about you. I'm guessing the friendship isn't *that* strong."

Tommy just shrugged.

She let out a faint breath. "Do you have an alibi?"

"I was breaking the law," he said with a nod.

She bit her lip. "Let me guess, the only people who could vouch for you won't."

"That's about right."

"Tommy!"

"Why fifteen years?"

She hesitated at the sudden change in conversation. His voice was still cold, his eyes like flint, but she knew her brother. Even after all this time, she knew Tommy Blythe. And he was sad. The hurt was evident in his tone, though, he endeavored to conceal it.

"Tommy, that's such a long conversation. Answer *my* questions. Do you have an alibi or not?"

"How about we make a deal, sis? You tell me why, and I'll answer. Never thought I'd see the day a Blythe joined law enforcement."

"I did not *join* them. They asked for my help." She decided not to mention the part about their father's involvement. "Let's start with yesterday. Where were you?"

"Here, around. I don't exactly have roommates, sis."

"Would you have been seen on your cameras?" she said, pointing at the monitors.

He shrugged. "Yeah, probably."

She felt a flash of relief. "Could you give me the footage? I can show it to the FBI, to clear your name."

He shook his head. "No good. It doesn't record. It's just so I can see if I get any trespassers."

Artemis' heart plummeted again. "Dammit, Tommy. I'm trying to help you." Her voice echoed in the strange, metallic space.

Tommy was shaking his head, his long hair swishing. "I don't need your help, but I want your answers. I'll talk if you do. Why haven't you been back?"

She glared at him. "Don't be ridiculous. I wanted to. I did but look at you. Look at all of this. I was nearly arrested for walking out of the crime scene. They hate us in Pinelake, Tommy. And you," she said, speaking faster and saying more than she had intended, "I mean, look at you. You just blew up a motorcycle. You were being chased by gunmen."

"Mild disagreement," he muttered.

"I don't even want to know. I never have. I've told you, how many times have I told you, you have to get out of this? Christ—you started, what... when you were twelve? Running packages, right? That's what you told Helen. Tommy, you're going to kill yourself, and I'm not willing to watch."

She shrugged, biting her lip and glancing off into a corner. She was surprised to find her voice shaky. No tears in her eyes. She still hadn't experienced these in more than a decade. But she knew, as she stood there, that she wasn't telling the whole truth. She didn't want to see her brother die. But she also didn't want to draw close. Not again. It was too painful. People left. People changed. The only constant was disappointment.

Her sister, dead; her father, a killer. Jamie Kramer, now acting strange and somehow in cahoots with the sheriff. She still wasn't sure he could be cleared of these crimes.

The Pinelake Police Department harassing her.

She supposed this last part wasn't so much a change as standard fare.

But at her core, she knew she couldn't do it again. Even when she had been sent to homes, shuttled from one place to the next, she felt as if pieces of her had been left behind. There were only so many people she could bond with, loves she could have, before it became too painful to keep trying.

In a few short years, her favorite person in the world, her sister, had been killed. Then her father had been arrested. They had lost the family home. Then she had lost her hometown. Then, as if that wasn't enough, she had been kicked out of the Kramer residence.

As she considered this, feeling her emotions rising, she scowled at her brother.

"You ran away," she snapped.

He blinked, staring at her.

She pointed a finger at his chest. "Don't blame me. You ran away. I lost everything. Everyone. And you left too."

She hadn't realized she was shouting, but now she couldn't hold back the words. She felt an irrational anger rising. "And now you've gone and taken a step off the deep end. Tommy, I don't even know who you are anymore."

"And you think that's my fault?" he shouted back. It was almost as if they'd *had* this conversation before, though Artemis knew they hadn't. But she'd rehearsed it so many times in her head, drifting off to sleep. And now, by the sound of things, it seemed as if Tommy had as well.

She shot back. "You're damn right I do. It *is* your fault. Your fault that I have to do this on my own. You didn't have to run away. You were my only friend. My only real friend."

"You had Jamie. Don't pretend like you two weren't sneaking off every moment you could get. You didn't need me."

She scowled. "I did. I lost everything too, Tommy. You're not the only one who suffered. You might think it's appropriate to go around taking your pain out on the world, living like one big middle finger but you're not the only one who was hurt. You're not the only person in the world, Tommy Blythe. Maybe no one ever told you that."

"Ha!" he said, jamming a finger towards the ceiling. "Even after all this time, you're still angry that I wasn't hoodwinked by dad."

"What? Don't be ridiculous."

"No, that's what this is. You're jealous. Jealous that I had a backup plan. I knew something was off with dad."

"Bullshit you did. None of us knew. You didn't know anything."

He shrugged. "I knew that he was making more money than he should've been. I would go through ticket sales every night. But by the time it showed up in the account, it would double."

She glared. None of them had been allowed access to the financial information. It made sense that, of all people, Tommy had found a way to snoop.

"You said you would answer my questions now. So go on. Give me an alibi. Tell me you weren't involved, Tommy. Look me in the eyes and tell me you're not a psychopath too."

He glared at her. Artemis was breathing heavily, realizing her hands were shaking. She wasn't so much scared as furious.

"Artemis," Tommy said slowly, his voice low, soft. He looked her dead in the eyes. "I swear, from the bottom of my heart," he said, unblinking, "I killed them. I killed every one of them. Murdered them. Dead. Dead. Dead. I had fun doing it too." He threw back his head and crowed, laughing at the ceiling, and waving his hands, as if he were seeing visions on the metal. "It was a riot. It was fun. I killed them dead, Artemis."

And then he looked back at her, glaring defiantly.

At first, she wanted to stalk across the room and slap him. Of course, he was lying. This, like always, was Tommy's twisted sense of humor.

"You're impossible," she muttered.

He smirked. "See, you don't believe I did it either. Stop being dumb."

"You're saying you didn't do it?" she insisted.

He shook his head. "I cut them open, smoked their ribs, and ate their faces. So what are you going to do about it? Leave again? Maybe you'll turn me in. Like you did dad."

"Hang on," she shouted, "you can't possibly blame me for that. That was his fault."

He looked away now, adjusting some of the blankets on the cardboard boxes. He muttered beneath his breath, and she leaned in, "What was that?"

"I said," he snapped, firmly, "it was your fat mouth that brought the cops to our house. You were the one who called that news station when you saw the detective identify the wrong car."

"I didn't know it was dad's car."

"You should've. Helen would have."

He went still now, and Artemis felt as if she'd been kicked. Silence reigned between the two of them now, and she wanted nothing more than to clamber up the metal ladder and storm out.

"Say it," she murmured, "Tommy, I mean it. Say it. Tell me you didn't do it."

"You know I didn't," he retorted. "I'm not saying shit. I don't owe you anything. I barely even recognize you. You've changed, Artemis. You shouldn't have come back. Now, get out of my house."

His voice shook with emotion. His back was still to her. But now, as she readied a retort of her own, her eyes were drawn to the monitors on the wall.

She stared, frowning and then going still.

Men and women in tactical gear and blue bulletproof vests displaying FBI in white letters were hastening through the old train yard. And leading the way, she recognized a tall, handsome man with bedraggled hair and a lumpy ear. Next to him, also in body armor, she spotted a woman with snow white hair, severe features, and a posture that suggested she had an iron rod in her spine. Next to the woman, came a man with a thick chest and broad shoulders, wearing sunglasses.

Agent Grant, Forester, and Wade were marching towards her brother's makeshift flat. And twenty SWAT accompanied them.

25

"Tommy," she said, her voice shaking.

"I mean it, get the hell out of here."

"No, Tommy, *look*."

He turned sharply, and his eyes widened. He stared at the screens, and then he looked at his sister. For a moment, the angry, irate criminal was gone. Instead, she remembered the young, scared boy, who had crept into her room the night Helen had gone missing. He had slept on the floor by her bed. In the end, she had given him her pillow and blankets. She could still remember his trembling voice. The same question, the same hurt.

This time, though, he was looking at her. "Why?"

"Tommy, I swear, I didn't call them. I was trying to avoid this."

He bit his lip and then snarled, and she watched as he pulled a weapon from inside his waistband, gripping it tightly.

"Tommy, hey," she said, urgently, "Don't. Come on, be serious. There's like twenty of them!"

But her brother gripped his weapon, his teeth set. The hurt, the betrayal in his face morphed quickly into rage.

For one moment, she thought he might even point the weapon at her. But he never did. Never even came close to doing it. He did, however, brush roughly past her, shoving her to the side, and stood facing the trapdoor, his weapon raised, his teeth set in an expression of defiance.

She stared at her brother, glanced at the monitors. Her voice shook. "Put it down. You're going to get yourself killed."

Forester was clambering on top of the train car first. They seemed to know exactly where they were going. She wondered in that horrible moment if they had been tracking her phone. Maybe she had gotten ahead of herself, thinking she could outsmart the FBI. They had been using her.

She cursed, ripping her phone from her pocket and glancing at it. She turned it off.

Not that it would matter anymore.

Forester and Wade were now on top of the metal container. She could hear their footsteps echoing through the space. Her brother was silent, his shoulders braced against the metal wall, his jacket stretched taut, his weapon held high.

Wade reached down. More FBI funneled to the top of the train car.

Someone was going to get killed. Her brother, certainly, another person, most likely.

"Tommy," she said, her voice shaking, "I swear I didn't mean to bring them here."

He didn't reply. Even in that moment, facing death, he was giving her the silent treatment.

The trapdoor began to open. Tommy's fingers braced on his trigger. He licked his lips nervously, tense.

And so Artemis did what she had to.

A wild swing. A quick *thunk*.

And the cast iron skillet from the propane stove collided with her brother's ponytail.

He toppled like a puppet with snipped strings.

She stared at where her brother lay on the ground, motionless. Hastily, she hurried forward, grabbed the gun, and hid it in her own waistband. No sense in having him brought up on weapons charges too. But she was moving on autopilot. The charges he faced were *far* more serious than some gun charge.

He didn't have an alibi. He was wearing the ring. He had ties to the mobster who had sold the gold. He had ties to the Kramer family. And now, standing there, trembling, she realized, perhaps more than anyone else besides her, Tommy had reason to hate Pinelake.

And then the trapdoor was flung open, light spewing through. Loud voices barking, "FBI! FBI!"

"Don't shoot!" she shouted back. "We're unarmed! Don't shoot! He's unconscious."

She watched as dark figures slipped through the ceiling, once they had determined the coast was clear.

She backed away, her shoulders shaking against the metal wall. The FBI streamed into her brother's hideout.

She had led them right to him. Tommy was already mad. Now she realized, with a sinking feeling, he was never going to forgive her.

Worse still, she wasn't sure if she even wanted him to. Had he killed those women? If not, she had just ruined her brother's life.

26

ARTEMIS SAT IN THE back of the police cruiser, watching as the two men argued. Forester had slipped her in the backseat without putting her in cuffs, while Tommy had been led away, once he'd come to consciousness, in cuffs.

She could still see the look on Tommy's face as he'd passed her. She swallowed, feeling that gaze of reproach cut deep. Fifteen years she hadn't returned. And the moment she did, she turned her brother in to the FBI.

Now, though, the locals had shown up.

And by the sound of things, they wanted custody of Artemis.

Forester was standing between Sheriff Dawkins, Ross Dawkins and three other deputies. The tall, lanky agent was shaking his head. "FBI case—FBI arrest. She's ours."

"My town!" the sheriff snapped.

"We're not in your town," Forester replied just as quickly.

Some more arguments continued, but at last, the sheriff and his men moved off, cursing Forester as they left.

Only then did Agent Forester slip back into the front seat of the vehicle. He put the car in gear quickly and pulled out of the dusty parking spot on the opposite side of the chain-link fence.

As he drove, he shot a look in the rearview mirror.

"Hey, Checkers," he said hesitantly. "Rough day?"

She scowled at him. "You tracked my phone."

"Tapped it too," he said. "We heard everything. Heard your brother admit it. Good job... Grant was impressed you had it in you... A bit... unwittingly albeit."

Artemis was still scowling. Forester shot her a sidelong look.

"He didn't do it," Artemis said firmly.

"You heard him. You heard what he shouted. He literally admitted to it. He had no alibi."

"I can't believe you tapped my phone," she said, glaring at him. She frowned, shifting in the seat, and twisting at the seatbelt. At least he hadn't cuffed her.

"Grant's idea." He shrugged. "She's a strong believer in *trust but verify.*"

Artemis watched as another vehicle pulled past them. A police car, veering far too close for comfort. Forester cursed, merging sharply into the left lane, and blaring the horn as the cop car sped away.

Like always, Forester moved at his own pace. He didn't try to keep up with the police car. Nor did he change the speed he traveled at. But the tall, lanky man frowned through the windshield.

"Tommy didn't do it," Artemis insisted. "He was being sarcastic."

"How do you know?"

"Because I know my brother."

"But it's been years. You haven't been back in a while, isn't that what you said? We heard him. Your brother, Artemis, has a long rap sheet. He's a violent criminal." Forester said all of this quickly, with no acid in his tone, as if he were simply commenting on the weather.

"He's never going to forgive me," Artemis murmured, staring out the window as they moved back towards the mountains, and gray asphalt turned to green foliage. Towards the top of the northern Cascades, she spotted pockets of snow beneath the clouds, at the very peaks, and trailing down the slopes.

Forester didn't comment on this last part. He maintained his lethargic speed, hovering just below the speed limit, and occasionally glancing towards notifications on his phone in the seat next to him.

"Where are they taking him?"

"Grant wants to interview him. Wade will be there. They'll want a confession."

Her fingers curled, scraping through the thin plastic layer on the inside of the window.

She knew her brother.

"Artemis?" Forester murmured.

"What?" she snapped.

He kept his tone patient. "What if he *did* do it?"

She scowled deeply then grimaced.

Her mind was at war with itself. She didn't know what to believe. On one side, as she considered it, she couldn't help but see things from the FBI's perspective. Tommy had connections to the mobster who had sold the gold. Tommy had a class ring.

Tommy had a violent criminal record. Tommy had reason to hate Pinelake.

But also... *it was her twin brother.*

He'd admitted it, yes... but sarcastically. She knew that voice, that tone. He'd been mocking her. Irritating, yes. But not incriminating.

"Maybe it won't make a difference," he said, "but I went through that yearbook you gave me. I checked every name."

She shot him a look. "And?"

"Alibis, out-of-state, one dead. It wasn't a very big football team, Artemis. Jamie Kramer was also on the list. But he was vouched for by the sheriff. They have security footage of him at the office."

Artemis let out a small breath of air. At least that meant Jamie was clear. She had hoped this would come with more relief, but she was too worried about her brother. Everything she touched just got worse.

She bit her lip, fidgeting uncomfortably. In her mind, she watched movements on a board, rehearsing them inaudibly, helping her focus, to calm. *D4. E6. E3. Knight C6.*

But even this memory trick didn't help. Tommy was now in FBI custody. Helen and Artemis had often joked this was how their brother would eventually end up. But Artemis had never wanted to be the cause of it.

She felt a flash of guilt and wanted to slip through the seat, through the floor, and just disappear.

"Am I under arrest too?" she said softly.

"No. I told them you knew I had tapped your phone. You were in on it."

She shot the tall man a sidelong glance. "Why?"

He looked back at her and shrugged. "You didn't kill them. He's your brother. I don't blame you for trying to have his back."

She frowned. "Are you really a sociopath?"

"Remember those ground rules? Don't psychoanalyze me."

Artemis knew she should feel relieved that she wasn't getting in trouble for keeping the FBI out of the loop, but really, she couldn't imagine feeling much worse. She thought back to what her brother had said.

Why he had run away from the Kramer house. She remembered his assumption at the start of their conversation.

"That why you back? Kramer?"

She frowned, considering his words. An assumption. He assumed he knew why she had returned. Assumptions could cost the game. Could cost the championship. Assumptions were only useful as shorthand. Proper strategy required anticipating all possible intentions from an opponent.

But maybe she was thinking too much like Tommy's sister.

She had just won the Seattle Open, hadn't she?

She had made a name for herself by not falling into assumptions.

They moved hastily forward, under a low chill coming in from the mountains. The sky was darkening, and the glimpse of snow on the slopes was obscured by the falling clouds.

But as she stared through the window, her mind spinning, Artemis began to frown. She had made assumptions too. She could think of at least two. But there had been others. She played back the conversations she had heard, or been privy to. Replaying them perfectly in her mind.

"He's making them pay," she said softly.

"What's that?"

"You don't have the right guy," she repeated. But now, her voice was mostly a murmur.

"I hope you're wrong," he replied. "If you're not, the real killer will kill again."

She had been thinking this very thing.

The killer wasn't done. Forester's words still echoed. What if she was wrong? Was she putting her faith in her brother for nothing? No. No, she knew Tommy. Besides, the motive didn't match. "Tommy is a thief," she said firmly. "He would've taken the jewelry."

"What?"

"The jewelry, on the bodies. The valuables. The money. He would've taken it. Why would he leave it behind? Look at where he lives. He needs the money. Look what he does for a living. You saw his rap sheet. He's a criminal. He wouldn't track down buried gold and leave it there."

As she spoke, she could see the look of hesitation forming on Forester's face.

"Where do you want me to drop you off?" was all he said.

She shook her head in frustration. The FBI was going to be no help. They thought they had outsmarted her, using her as a tool to trap her own brother. But they were wrong. Tommy wouldn't kill those women. It would have been impossible for him not to take jewelry. Her brother always had sticky fingers.

Jamie was apparently cleared by footage. Which meant she was completely off. The ring. She was off about the ring. Jamie had said he'd lost it. Or let someone borrow it. But who would want to borrow a fake ring made of cheap materials from a junior varsity game?

And suddenly it hit her like a load of bricks.

Her mind was spinning. Pieces moving in place, strategy materializing. Tactics brushed aside in place of clear observation. She knew the assumptions that had been made. And now, sitting there, she realized the only way to help Tommy was to catch the real killer. But he was going to strike again. It was getting late. He was going to kill. And in the meantime, the FBI was barking up the wrong tree.

She shot a look at Forester. The man had tapped her phone. No. She would have to find proof. She would have to show them, for certain, that Tommy wasn't guilty. They would never take her word for it. She was related, after all.

Assumptions.

It all came down to assumptions.

"Forget the hotel," she said quickly, breathless. "I need you to drop me off somewhere else."

Forester shot her a look, raising an eyebrow questioningly.

She considered the pattern. Considered the pieces she was missing. It made sense. In fact, it was the only thing that made sense.

She had to find proof. Theory, speculation, was nothing.

Assumptions.

Maybe it wasn't too late after all, to save her brother. To save the killer's next target.

But for this to work, she first had to discover who the target was.

And now, she realized slowly, she knew exactly how to find out.

27

Artemis moved back up the mountain trail. Pine-needles and dust scattered with each footfall. Her heart pounded as she moved beneath the shifting branches above, the leaves and boughs whispering as if sharing some illicit secret.

She wondered if the trees could talk, what secrets they might murmur in her ears. Once, years ago, they'd witnessed her first kiss.

But these slopes were bathed in more than innocence. Other things lurked in the dark.

Her father had killed in these mountains. She moved up the trail, through the woods, frowning as she did. In her mind's eye, she pictured the small, plastic bottle she'd spotted when arguing with Jamie earlier in the day.

She'd been distracted by her fear. Distracted by the sudden horror of the moment.

But Jamie had been right. *You can see for miles from here. Can see... everything.*

You could see everything. And from the vantage point, a bit higher, where she'd spotted the empty bottle...

One might see further still, over the trees, down the slopes, in the direction of the large, looming mansions. She couldn't be sure if she'd made a mistake.

Oftentimes, this was how it felt in a tournament. Especially after a risky move. A gambit.

In a gambit, often, a piece would be sacrificed in order to find a winning position. She was now that piece. Not so much a queen, but more like a bishop, always looking for some new angle.

She came to a halt where the picnic blanket had been left discarded and crumpled. She inhaled the chilly night air. The mountain slopes were casting fog... Above, in the snow, she thought she could just make out the faint outline of frost.

She stared at the rocky terrace above the picnic spot, breathing slowly and summoning resolve.

And now, she reached out, grabbing at a mossy stone. She heaved a breath, rising up the side of the rocky outcrop. Her fingers tensed, digging into the soft, green padding. Stones skipped past her feet as she rose. The scent of the earth lingered in her nostrils. The rough stone grazed against knuckles, against her cheek and against her shoes as she climbed higher.

The clouds had pulled across the moon, hiding most the forest now. Only faint glimpses of lunar glow crept across the sky.

With a final heave, and a faint grunt, she managed to pull onto the rocky outcrop. Her fingers hit something plastic, sending it skittering. She frowned, her eyes settling on the pine-needle-strewn ground of the outcrop.

Bottles.

At least thirty of them scattered in the leaves. She wrinkled her nose, staring at the arrangement.

She glanced over her shoulder now, back down at the trail she'd come from. But the trail wasn't visible now at the angle she'd ascended to. Behind her... nestled in one corner of a stone platform was the first glimpses of mountain frost. And there, a small, wooden cabin.

She frowned at the old, worn cabin. It hadn't been used in years... At least... not when she'd been in the area. But now... a faint smattering of snow had covered the roof.

A strange thing to stand on rocky, chill ground and then a few paces away to see the first glimpses of frost.

Half snow, half mountain. The terrain at her feet was a strange juxtaposition. The further the mountains climbed, the more the snow thickened.

She shivered now, exhaling faintly. No movement in that small cabin... At least, none she could see.

Other things, however, *did catch* her eye. She turned slowly, staring down from the chilly slopes to peer far into the valley.

Mansions. The homes in the base of the valley, past the tall trees… From this vantage point, through a gap in two of the rising firs, posted like sentries standing against the wind, she spotted Mrs. Kramer's home.

And there, two doors down, Ms. Ortega's.

Across the road, on the small, three-acre lot, she noted the home of Mrs. Burrows, the first victim. No sign of Janet Tillman's home… Ms. Tillman lived at the end of a cul-de-sac hidden beyond a sloping hill.

Another thing caught her attention. The Kramer's house was slanted off to the side. While the backyard was mostly visible, the windows faced away from the mountain slopes.

She hesitated, considering the implications.

Her own words returned to her, slowly, like goosebumps.

He's making them pay.

Making them pay. The money, the gold, the expensive boat, the opulent house. All signs of luxury. But… She frowned, letting out a faint sigh.

Not just luxury. Making them pay…

Vengeance.

He wasn't killing for fun. Not like her father. This killer was hunting women for revenge. Artemis didn't know Pinelake how she once had.

Didn't know the people as well as she once had. Part of her wished she'd never returned.

But now, as she stared down from the vantage point strewn with plastic bottles, she tried to piece it all together.

She had a new perspective.

A higher perspective.

So what did it tell her? The killer was hunting women out of a sense of retribution... It didn't make sense yet. She let out a fluttering, little breath, wondering what Helen might have said. Her sister had always been the smarter one.

Artemis sat on the mossy stone, her fingers pressing into the vegetative cushion. Her eyes moved to the many discarded bottles circling the base of the protruding stone. Had this been the killer's vantage point? He had been watching his victims, and Artemis knew opponents like this. She once had played a game where her opponent had taken nearly an hour on a single move. As if he been studying every possible angle. But his next ten moves had come quickly, all under five seconds.

The hour of thinking had allowed him to act quickly subsequently.

Players like that were dangerous at the start of their blitz. But later on, the further out, the less time they had to calculate. They couldn't anticipate every move, and so sometimes, when moving pieces too rapidly, they would become carried away by their own emotions, their sense of urgency, their pride, hoping to keep the impression of omniscience.

The only question left, she thought, was where had the killer made his mistake?

Her brother was in jail now, being interrogated by Grant and Wade. Tommy had no alibi.

The mobster at the jewelry store had said Mr. and Mrs. Kramer had purchased gold, and then a man wearing Jamie's school ring had shown up asking about it...

But no.

No that wasn't exactly right, was it?

The *words* were right.

But assumptions had been made.

Artemis went very still now, running through the conversation with the mobster who'd spoken in broken English. It felt like she was analyzing a game. Felt like she was going over moves she'd already made.

Assumptions.

He *had* said Mr. and Mrs. Kramer had purchased the gold.

Artemis frowned...

What he'd *actually* said had been:

"Woman and man come in and buy gold."

And in response, Forester had asked.

"Mr. and Mrs. Kramer?"

The man had seemed to agree. Mr. and Mrs. Kramer... the phrasing hadn't been the jeweler's first instinct.

She hesitated a second...

And then her skin prickled in horrifying realization.

And suddenly, behind her, she heard movement.

Artemis twisted sharply, staring into the dark. The mountain slopes were creased with gaps and old stones. She frowned, staring into the dark.

Another sound... Difficult to determine the source due to the acoustics of the place.

She pulled out her phone with a trembling hand, raising it and turning the flashlight through the trees. The wind continued to rustle the branches. Boughs creaked and moaned.

And then she heard footsteps.

Unmistakably, the sound of rapid movement. Someone was below her. Someone was coming towards the outcrop.

She turned off her light hastily. Had the person seen her?

Was this... was this *him*?

Hastily, she pressed her phone against her leg, hiding the light from view. Her finger scrambled along the glass of the screen, desperately trying to dial 9-1-1.

But too late.

A face had appeared over the rocky outcrop, staring right at her.

28

The hand pressed against the stone was wearing a large, clunky ring with fake diamonds and a big, red bead of jeweler's glass in the center. A number six was carved in the side.

She stared in horror at the ring. Jamie had insisted he'd lost it… or that he'd let someone borrow it years ago. Now it was clear; someone had borrowed it. The only person who would have seen any value in a fake, jeweler's glass football ring for a junior varsity team. And then her eyes lifted as the face followed. At first, like a disembodied head, rising over the slope. But then, the rest of the figure followed.

She scrambled back, still desperately pressing buttons on her phone. But she was shaking so badly, she dropped the device. She bent over, snatching it up again.

"I gave my word," the man on the edge of the cliff whispered. His voice shook with emotion. His eyes were fixed on her. He wore a ski-mask, disguising his features. He pulled himself to his full height, stepping towards her, avoiding the scattered bottles with practiced ease. He'd been up here before.

"Wait!" she said sharply. "Wait, don't!"

But he kept coming towards her, his eyes blazing behind that mask.

They were alone, only the woods and the wind watching now. No other witnesses. The large homes at the base of the mountain wouldn't see a thing amidst the trees. No one could help. She tried screaming.

Would anyone hear?

"Quiet," he said sharply. "Don't make me hurt you worse than I already have to."

He reached towards her with one hand, holding the ring. She continued to scramble back, stumbling. But she nearly fell over the edge of the cliff, nearly tumbled off the rocky outcrop. A quick glance back told her this wasn't an option. On this side of the outcrop, she was facing a twenty-foot fall against sharp stones.

She glanced back as the man in the dark mask strolled slowly towards her, his motions and movements suggesting he had all the time in the world.

Fifteen feet. Ten.

He closed the distance, his footsteps occasionally sending a bottle skittering at his feet.

She wasn't a fighter like Forester. She wasn't a blood and guts, leave it all on the field scrapper like her brother Tommy. Artemis used her mind. Used pieces on a board game.

But she had no pieces left. No surprises. No upper hand.

None except one.

And so she played the only card she had. "I-I know who you are! Mr. Kramer—I know it's you!"

He went suddenly still. Only five feet away, frowning at her. In one hand, he clutched a gleaming knife as long as her forearm. And then, slowly, he reached up, tugging at the ski-mask. As he removed it, he murmured, "That was getting tiresome anyway. Not that it matters. You won't tell a soul."

And then she found herself staring at the older Kramer. Erik wasn't quite as handsome as his son, but he did have symmetrical features and bright eyes set above sharp cheekbones. His jaw was weaker though, his chin too small. He tried to compensate by growing a chin strap, but the facial hair was too patchy, speckled mostly with silver and gray.

Erik Kramer stared at Artemis Blythe, and he was frowning now, his eyes fixed on her. "Did you recognize me?" he murmured, tilting his head slowly to the side, standing within arm's reach of her.

Her words had their intended effect. They had bought Artemis a few more precious seconds. So she kept going, despite her terror, despite the trembling in her voice. "No... No, it was the only thing that made sense." She pointed off towards Kramer's own home. "You can't see through the windows on that one."

"Excuse me?" he said.

She'd been hoping he would look where she'd pointed. But he was staring right at her, unblinking. He kept hold of his knife, cradling it against his chest like a mother with a swaddled infant. Artemis couldn't help but swallow every time she glanced at the enormous blade. She didn't want to think how it might feel for it to jam into her ribs, to slash at her throat.

She tottered on the edge of the rocky outcrop, sending pebbles and dust skipping beneath her heels towards the ground twenty feet below. She took a hesitant step to the left, trying to improve her vantage point.

"Don't!" he said sharply. A harsh, cold voice. She remembered that voice. The same one he'd used when he'd ordered his wife to send Artemis away. This was a man accustomed to being obeyed.

He was now pointing his knife at her, and he stepped suddenly closer, the blade touching against her neck. Cold steel against soft flesh. She held her breath, staring down at the knife. Her eyes found his, and she realized there was a strange look on his face. His lips were twitching as if holding a smile. His eyes unblinking as he stared at the way his blade traced against the smooth skin of her throat.

"So very lovely," he murmured. "You were always sweet on Jamie. I can see why he was fond of you."

She felt chills down her neck. The knife pressed a bit harder.

She spoke again, rapidly, desperately searching for *something* to say. "You were the one who went to the gold-dealer! The man and woman who purchased the gold were your wife and *your son!* Mr. and Mrs. Kramer." An assumption. The jeweler, in broken English, had failed to clarify the first visitors *hadn't* been husband and wife. But mother and son. Jamie had gone with his mother to help buy the gold from the dealer recommended by his friend, Tommy.

It made sense now. And then two days later... Erik had come, demanding to know who bought the gold... but why? It didn't make sense. Did it?

Erik snorted at her. He wasn't limping, clearly suggesting the use of his walking cane had been a ruse. The sort of ruse... her own father might have cooked up.

He stared past her for the moment, eyes on the small, run-down cabin under the first touch of frost. His voice carried a similar, chilly cadence. "I saw the Ghostkiller's work up here... years ago, you know. I found the first body. The first girl..." He smiled at her now as he spoke, his skin sickly, pale. Jamie had mentioned his father had cancer...

This last comment was *not* what she'd been expecting. Artemis went cold, staring. Her fingers were still shaking horribly. Her breath came in ragged and rapid puffs of terror.

"I visited your father in prison, you know," he said softly, his voice hoarse. "He didn't have... No—no I hadn't seen it. Not at first. I spoke to the Ghostkiller. And that..." he coughed, his knife shaking. "That was where I found the path. Don't you see? The Ghostkiller helped me plan. Helped me execute. I couldn't have done this without the sheer *genius*—"

"He's not that smart," Artemis snapped, shaking horribly. This, she realized, was how her father had known about the case. He *hadn't* been lying. Mr. Kramer had visited the old charlatan in prison.

"Oh?" Kramer leered. "Not so smart? He's the one who knew that if I told Jamie the truth, I'd protect his heart... His mother..." Kramer swallowed. "She had to go... had to, don't you see? And when I told Jamie how his mother had been lying, sleeping around... I inoculated him against pain! It was brilliant. So brilliant. Ha—I even told a little white lie to help."

Artemis stared, then murmured, "You lied about whose idea it was to send me away..."

"Barely a lie," Kramer said, his voice rasping. "Barely... For his own sake. I've always loved my boy... He... he took it hard when I told Donna you couldn't stay. Took it very hard. But..." Kramer shook his head. "A little white lie helped inoculate the pain. In a way... his mother *was* the cause of our misery. Don't you see that?"

She thought back to when she'd seen Erik in his backyard... his shoulders shaking as he'd stared at the hole in his yard where his wife had been buried.

Weeping, she'd thought...

But what if he'd just been laughing?

Assumptions. And now she'd wandered too close to the wolf's den.

"See that?" he said conversationally now, pointing off with a finger. "One of my little projects... No—look. Look!" he roared suddenly, rage bursting forth.

She complied quickly, staring past his shaking hand gripping the bright knife. He indicated the valley. Towards the house across from the Ortega's.

And that's when she spotted it.

Far, far below, a small, dark silhouette shifting and writhing on the roof, near the chimney. She leaned in, momentarily confused. The figure continued to kick and buck and thrash.

Erik was giggling now. "A noose around the chimney. Legs weighted with platinum bars I found in the safe. Not that I have any use for platinum where I'm going—cancer has a way of reorienting, you know. But her? She's slowly going to hang... An hour, two... No one will see a thing. No one does in this town, do they?"

She stared at the woman being hung from the chimney, her protests cut off by the rope around her neck. But she couldn't climb back to safety due to the weights tied to her ankles. And so she continued to kick and thrash.

"See it?" he whispered at her. "When she tires... when exhaustion sets in, she won't be able to fight it. How long do you think Ms. Ackroyd will last?"

Artemis knew Ackroyd's name. She'd been in that same house for nearly twenty years. The woman had always been pleasant and kind to Artemis and her brother... until the news had broken. Then, at least, she'd gone quiet instead of vengeful.

"They're cheats," Erik whispered, nodding. "All of them."

"Who-who is?" she said, shaking horribly.

"The bitches I dusted," he screamed suddenly. He took another step towards her, and now she nearly toppled off the cliff. Her arms windmilled, keeping her from falling.

"I gave my life to that woman! My *life*!" he yelled. "And what do I find? Hmm... At my lowest, after my damn diagnosis—" He paused, coughing again, bending double. "I find her *cheating* on me. And who with? Not another man—no..." He pointed the knife accusingly over the cliff, towards the chimney.

"I've watched them... all of them for so long. I never thought to watch my own damn house. You're right—the windows don't face us. But the others—Ortega was sleeping with a pool boy. How cliché, yes? And that bitch next door was seducing her sister's husband."

"You—you've been murdering the unfaithful?"

"Justice!" He screamed at her. "Not murder—justice! Donna deserved it. She thought she was clever, buying that gold. All heirlooms go to her in case of a divorce! Her father's idea. I didn't care at the time. But the gold falls under the category. She used my own sweet... sweet boy..." his voice shook, his hand with the ring trembling. "To buy the gold without me knowing. I went to find out how much they'd bought. The idiot at the store attacked me! The savage."

Artemis just stared, trying to make sense of it. Jamie had been angry at his mother not long after the gold purchase, though. "You told Jamie," she whispered. "Told him his mother was cheating."

"I did—I've always loved my boy, and..." his voice cracked, "And *she* had to go and ruin everything."

"You're dying!" Artemis insisted, still precarious on the ledge. "You're dying, yes?" She kept shooting panicked glances towards the woman dangling from the chimney. She was still fighting, still holding the rope, not yet spent. But time was passing, even the kicking motions, the desperate struggle of the dying woman was fleeting.

"Gold," he whispered. "Jewelry. It was the Ghostkiller's idea to kill Donna later. So that they wouldn't look at me first! Also the Ghostkiller's idea to bury them with gold, jewelry. To make them pay for their crimes! They are given *everything*!" he screamed at her. "And *this* is how they repay me?"

Now spittle flecked her cheek. Artemis could feel her heart pounding horribly. The woman dangling from the chimney was no longer struggling as much. Artemis, though, had her own demise to worry about. If she fell now... chances of survival were grim at best.

Mr. Kramer paused, his arm still outstretched, one hand reaching towards her as if to grab her by the shirt, or perhaps caress her hair. His posture was difficult to interpret now. Clearly—pupils delighted, breathing irregularly—he was both excited and enjoying himself.

Now his other hand grabbed her arm, holding it in a limp-wristed sort of way. This was not a strong man. His touch felt more... tender than violent.

This only added a note of revulsion to her fear.

"I'm supposed to give you a message," he said. He leaned in. "Helen isn't dead," he whispered in her ear.

And then he slammed the knife towards her stomach.

Artemis panicked, did the only thing she could think of. She dropped to the ground, the knife slicing over her. Erik Kramer screamed, slashing down with his knife at her back, and she grabbed the only item available to defend herself.

One of the plastic bottles.

The knife cut straight through the center. And Kramer screamed, kicking at her. The killer yanked his blade from the bottle, raised it high and with a scream he—

Bang! Bang!

Two quick retorts from over by the trail leading up the mountain. Mr. Kramer blinked, stumbling. Blood pooled down his chest, spilling now in red streams. He stared at Artemis, briefly, tilting his head curiously. And then he toppled backwards, hitting the ground. His knife clattering free.

She stared, breathing heavily, her eyes fixated on his form.

A twitch. A groan.

Then silence.

"Artemis?" Forester shouted from the forest floor. "Are you alright?"

"Thank God you got my message!" she shouted back, breathing in rapid pants. She leaned back, glancing towards the floor. There, standing on the picnic blanket, Agent Cameron Forester still held his gun gripped tight. He'd just shot a man, but his hands weren't trembling. Nothing about his posture suggested any sort of discomfort.

"He down?"

"He's down," she said, urgently, double-checking.

He called up. "I saw you texted me. Was just numbers but the tap was still live. Good thing you—"

"Forester!" she shouted. "Ms. Ackroyd. Across the street—she's on the roof. Please! Send someone!"

"Shit," he said, as he peered in the direction she was pointing over the lip of the rocky outcrop.

"Backup is on the street," he said. "I'm calling it in. Are you good for a sec?"

She nodded slowly, breathing in gasps, motionless on the edge of the rock and staring towards the chilly cabin a bit further up the slope. And now she remembered the spot.

The location where her father had killed his first victim...

And she also remembered what Erik Kramer had said... The Ghostkiller, her old man, had given a message. A knife in the dark... but also...

Helen was still alive...

He'd said it before, though... hadn't he?

Taunting, playing. Just more of his games.

Kramer was no longer moving

Forester was rapidly shouting instructions into his phone. Artemis glimpsed the flare of red and blue lights against the Ackroyd residence's windows.

She kept glancing towards the small cabin. The site of her father's first kill. And now... by the sound of things, he had helped Mr. Kramer plan and execute the murders.

She felt a flash of rage.

But this simmered down as she lay there, gasping at the night sky, inhaling the frigid air shed by the higher slopes.

She'd been right.

Tommy hadn't done it.

Jamie was innocent.

She'd been right.

29

ARTEMIS SHIFTED UNEASILY IN the borrowed vehicle outside the police department. Her brother had been in FBI custody, so at least the locals wouldn't have had a chance to get at him.

Plus, with the news breaking of the *actual* killer, shot by Forester, even the Dawkins' had less reason to actively antagonize the Blythes.

Now, though, she watched as Tommy moved through the doors of the precinct, his hair draping his shoulders, his ever-present saunter accompanying a shifting, leather jacket tossed over his shoulder.

As he marched down the sidewalk, moving towards her, Artemis breathed slowly, then lowered the window.

She half expected him to just walk past.

She winced, and said, hesitantly, "I—I can give you a ride. Anywhere you want."

He paused, his eyes flicking towards her.

She spotted faces in the windows, staring out at the curb. A few officers lingered by their vehicles in the parking lot, studying the figures.

Tommy ignored all of them. He just watched Artemis.

"I found the real killer," she said. "I found him. To help you. I really, really didn't know they had my phone tapped. I swear, Tommy."

He just kept staring at her.

She scowled back now. "Dammit, alright. I'm sorry! Fifteen years was too long. I... I know that. I'm sorry."

He brushed some of his long hair out of his face, still standing on the sidewalk. He hadn't walked away—at least there was that.

"What do you *want* from me?" she muttered. She paused though, glancing past Tommy. Agent Forester had emerged in the doorway. The lanky fed had been the one to help get Tommy cut loose so quickly.

"It true you saved Ackroyd?" Tommy suddenly said.

Artemis nodded quickly. Then paused, waved a hand. "Some cop did the saving, but... but I helped get them to her in time. She's bruised but is going to live."

"Jamie's dad? That true too?"

Artemis winced. "He... look, how about you get in, and we can talk. I'll take you anywhere."

"You leaving again?" Tommy said, frowning.

Forester was watching from the open door to the precinct. Grant was nowhere to be seen. Artemis shifted uncomfortably. She didn't know where Jamie Kramer was. She wondered how he was taking the news. What was it about this place? Seattle was often called the serial killer capital of the U.S. There was a far larger percentage of killers in the misty Northwest.

But it was Kramer's diagnosis, his wife's infidelity that had broken him. He'd given in to an evil man's whispers. He'd sought out the Ghostkiller in prison. Forester had already checked the records. Mr. Kramer had visited her father only once, a few months before.

She let out a faint sigh, looking away from Agent Forester. Away from the police station. Her eyes settled on her brother.

"I... I have a tournament I'm going to prepare for," she said slowly. "I've got to."

He nodded. "You can do that local."

She huffed. "It almost sounds like you want me to stay."

"I *wanted* you to stay back then," he said sharply. "I'm not a teenager anymore, sis."

She hesitated, considering his words. She'd been mulling over, all morning, what she might end up doing. She knew she couldn't ignore what she'd been told by Kramer.

Helen isn't dead.

Her father was toying with them. That was all.

Then again...

She bit her lip.

Only one person would *truly* know. Her old man.

"I'm going to visit him," she said quietly.

"What?"

"Dad. I'm going to visit him in prison. Next week. It's already scheduled."

Tommy stared at her.

"So... so I guess I'll be around for a week, at least," she winced. "Tommy, really. I promise I didn't mean—"

He was rounding the hood now though; approached the side, flung open the door, and slipped in. The door shut again with a loud *thud*.

"Chicken nuggets," he said simply. "You hungry?"

She blinked, staring at her brother. He wasn't smiling. Tommy rarely smiled.

But Artemis brushed her dark hair behind an ear, pulling it back into the band of her simple ponytail. Nationals would be next month. She'd earned a slot after winning in Seattle.

A week from now, though, she would sit across from the Ghostkiller...

He was lying about Helen.

He had to be…

She glanced at Tommy, opening her mouth.

"What?" he said, frowning.

She closed it again. "N-nothing. Umm, yeah—sure. Chicken sounds great. I could use some grease and a premature heart attack."

Tommy snorted, flashed a thumbs up, and leaned back, throwing his feet on the dash.

Sometimes it seemed impossible they'd been born on the same day.

But at least he'd agreed to the ride.

Baby steps.

She glanced back towards the precinct. Forester was waving now. A slow, almost sarcastic flutter of his hand.

"That guy's a tool," Tommy muttered.

"Yeah," Artemis agreed. "He did save my life last night, though."

"Shit. Real?"

"Yeah… I can tell you all about it on the way. Look—could you buckle up, please?"

"Nah."

She sighed and didn't even bother asking a second time.

The End

WHAT'S NEXT FOR ARTEMIS BLYTHE?

SHE HIDES FOREVER

Chessmaster and FBI consultant, Artemis Blythe, will have to keep her wits about her as she visits her old man, the Ghostkiller, in prison.

A notorious murderer who targeted seven women in the sleepy town of Pinelake.

Artemis only wants one thing: to discover if her sister, Helen, is still alive.

But her father is making moves of his own. And now, outside the walls of the prison, a giant of a killer is drowning the daughters of powerful men...

Artemis pits her wits against her father, this new killer, and anyone else in town who scorns her family name.

ALSO BY GEORGIA WAGNER

GIRL UNDER THE ICE

Once a rising star in the FBI, with the best case closure rate of any investigator, Ella Porter is now exiled to a small gold mining town bordering the wilderness of Alaska. The reason for her

new assignment? She allowed a prolific serial killer to escape custody.

But what no one knows is that she did it on purpose.

The day she shows up in Nome, bags still unpacked, the wife of the richest gold miner in town goes miss-ing. This is the second woman to vanish in as many days. And it's up to Ella to find out what happened.

Assigning Ella to Nome is no accident, either. Though she swore she'd never return, Ella grew up in the small, gold mining town, treated like royalty as a child due to her own family's wealth. But like all gold ty-coons, the Porter family secrets are as dark as Ella's own.

Once a hypnotist with her own TV show, now, Sophie Quinn works as a full-time consultant for the FBI. Everything changed six years ago. She can still remember that horrible night. Slated to be the River Killer's tenth victim, she managed to slip her bindings and barely escape where so many others failed. Her sister wasn't so lucky.

And now the killer is back.

Two PHDs later, she's now a rising star at the FBI. Her photographic memory helps solve crimes, but also helps her to never forget. She saw the River Killer's tattoo. She knows what he sounds like. And now, ten years later, he's active again.

Sophie Quinn heads back home to the swamps of Louisiana, along the Mississippi River, intent on evening the score and finding the man who killed her sister. It's been six years since she's been home, though. Broken relationships and shattered dreams exist among the bayous, the rivers, the waterways and swamps of Louisiana; can Sophie find her way home again? Or will she be the River Killer's next victim to float downstream?

Want to Know More?

GREENFIELD PRESS IS THE brainchild of bestselling author Steve Higgs. He specializes in writing fast paced adventurous mystery and urban fantasy with a humorous lilt. Having made his money publishing his own work, Steve went looking for a few 'special' authors whose work he believed in.

Georgia Wagner was the first of those, but to find out more and to be the first to hear about new releases and what is coming next, you can join the Facebook group by clicking the link below. Or copying the

following link into your browser - www.facebook.com/GreenfieldP
ress.

ABOUT THE AUTHOR

Georgia Wagner worked as a ghost writer for many, many years before finally taking the plunge into self-publishing. Location and character are two big factors for Georgia, and getting those right allows the story to flow seamlessly onto the page. And flow it does, because Georgia is so prolific a new term is required to describe the rate at which nerve-tingling stories find their way into print.

When not found attached to a laptop, Georgia likes spending time in local arboretums, among the trees and ponds. An avid cultivator of orchids, begonias, and all things floral, Georgia also has a strong penchant for art, paintings, and sculptures. A many-decades long passion for mystery novels and years of chess tournament experience makes Georgia the perfect person to pen the Artemis Blythe series.